BREAKING TIES

DELTA FORCE STRONG BOOK #6

ELLE JAMES

TWISTED PAGE INC

BREAKING TIES

DELTA FORCE STRONG BOOK #6

New York Times & *USA Today*
Bestselling Author

ELLE JAMES

AUTHOR'S NOTE

Enjoy other military books by Elle James

Delta Force Strong
Ivy's Delta (Delta Force 3 Crossover)
Breaking Silence (#1)
Breaking Rules (#2)
Breaking Away (#3)
Breaking Free (#4)
Breaking Hearts (#5)
Breaking Ties (#6)
Breaking Point (#7)
Breaking Dawn (#8)

Visit ellejames.com for titles and release dates
For hot cowboys, visit her alter ego Myla Jackson
at mylajackson.com
and join Elle James's Newsletter at
https://ellejames.com/contact/

PROLOGUE

"I GOT A BOGEY AT TWO O'CLOCK," Dawg whispered into his headset. Doug "Dawg" Masters lay low in the underbrush, his night vision goggles trained on the small compound thirty yards from his position.

"Got a truck coming in from the west," Rucker reported. "Looks like it's loaded with armed men. Estimate eight to ten plus the driver and passenger. ETA three minutes. Any sign of our target?"

"Not yet." On point, Dawg was the closest to the compound and had the best vantage point. Movement from the central hut caught his attention. "Wait. Got people coming out now."

"Kalani?"

"Hard to say in the dark. Three…four…five men, and they seem to be gathered around the one in the middle."

"Kalani," Rucker stated. "Be ready to move."

The team responded, one by one. "Ready."

"Lance, Tank and I will hold off the incoming," Rucker said. "The rest of you know the plan. Let's do this."

The team moved in under the concealment of night, each equipped with either an M4A1 rifle with the SOPMOD upgrades or small machineguns.

Their mission was to take out an important leader of the Boko Haram, a man responsible for the latest rash of kidnappings of school children they held for ransom. The last raid had netted one hundred and twenty girls from a boarding school and had cost the parents and government a lot of money. The Deltas wouldn't have been involved if the raid hadn't also involved killing several American school teachers in the process. One of the teachers had been the daughter of a New York senator.

The powers that be in Washington wanted to send the Islamic State faction a message by way of taking out one of their most prominent leaders.

Which was why Dawg and his team of Delta Force operatives were neck deep in the brush and up to their eyeballs in bad guys. Their advantage? Boko Haram didn't know they were there or that anyone would actually target them. They had the northeast area of the African country so afraid of them they met little resistance.

That was about to come to an abrupt end.

"Going in." Ryan "Dash" Hayes moved the fastest of all of them. Because he was so fast, he was their point man moving forward.

"I've got your six," Sean McDaniels's voice sounded in Dawg's ear. Mac was an excellent shot. He'd make certain Dash was covered on his way in.

Blade would move in at the same time from his position with Dawg providing fire support until Blade got ahead of him. The team would leapfrog closer until they were near enough to launch their strike.

"Blade going in," Blade said into the radio.

"Bull going in," Bull said.

"Gotcha," Dawg said. "I'm right behind you."

As soon as Blade and Bull made it past him and hunkered low in the tall grass surrounding the compound, Dawg left his position. Hunched low to the ground, he ran forward until he reached the corner of one of the huts.

"Dash is in position," Mac reported.

"Dawg, Bull and Blade are too," Blade whispered.

Dawg held his silence and raised his rifle to his shoulder. He and Dash had M4A1 rifles with noise suppression devices. Their best bet was to take out the leader while he stood outside. The people around him would immediately fall back and take cover inside the building. The trick was to hit their target before the leader made it back into the building.

Cutting off the head of the snake would slow the Boko Haram movement. The team knew it wouldn't last for long. The US government hoped the strike would send a message to others of the Islamic State movement that their continued terrorism against the children of Nigeria would not be tolerated by the rest of the world.

Dawg hoped the leaders in Washington were right but doubted that Boko Haram would stop laying siege against the children, farmers and herders in Nigeria as long as the jihadists were alive and breathing.

As Dawg sighted in on his target, an SUV rumbled across the gravel toward the group of terrorists gathered around Kalani. Then a man stepped between Dawg and the terrorist leader. "I don't have a clear shot," he whispered.

"I do," Dash said.

"Take it before the SUV reaches them," Rucker ordered.

As Dash fired off his round, the group shifted again, giving Dawg a clear view of the leader.

The man between Kalani and Dash jerked and fell to the ground.

Dawg pulled his trigger. The bullet left the rifle's chamber and hit the target a moment later.

The group of men still standing dove for the

building, shouting. One of them grabbed Kalani as he slumped, dragged him through the doorway and slammed it shut behind them.

Dawg cursed. He'd aimed straight for Kalani's heart. If the man had moved even slightly before the bullet reached him, he could survive. If he did, he'd use the incident as a war cry and proof that he was the chosen one to intensify the jihadist movement until all the infidels were annihilated from the earth.

The team moved in.

Gunfire sounded to the west where Rucker, Tank and Lance held off the truck full of terrorists.

More terrorists emerged from surrounding buildings, wielding AK-47s and machine guns.

Before long, the night was alight with gunfire and men shouting. If the team hadn't been prepared, the confusion would have been overwhelming.

While Dawg, Mac and Blade covered, Dash ran forward, kicked in the door of the central building. He tossed in a fragment grenade and dove to the side, covering his ears.

Dawg ducked and covered his ears.

Boom!

The front wall blasted outward, spewing a cloud of dust and debris.

The men who'd emerged from the nearby huts

picked themselves up off the ground and fired into the night indiscriminately.

One by one, Dawg and his team picked them off.

The SUV that had been headed toward the central building spun gravel up from its back tires as the driver raced toward the road leading out of the compound and toward Rucker, Lance and Tank's positions.

"Got one making a run for it," Dawg said into his mic.

"On our radar," Rucker responded.

The sharp report of gunfire continued, but the SUV plowed through the gauntlet of Deltas, swerving right then left. The windshield was blown out, but the driver kept moving until he was out of range.

"Damn," Rucker muttered into the mic. "Gather what intel you can find. I'm calling for extraction."

"Roger," Dawg said.

The team moved in, conducting a swift sweep of the area and collecting anything that might be used by the intelligence guys.

With Bull covering for them, Dawg, Dash and Mac entered the blown-out building and dragged the bodies of the men inside into the open for iden-tification. They took photos of the dead.

"Is it Kalani?" Dash asked.

Dawg nodded. "Looks like him." He brushed his

finger across the man's dusty face and nodded. "He's got the scar on his left eyebrow."

"It's him," Mac said. "He had a gap between his front teeth, too. This guy has it."

"We've got another truckload of fun coming our way," Rucker said. "Time to bug out."

The team converged outside the east side of the compound at the predesignated pickup point.

A Black Hawk helicopter swooped in and landed just long enough for the men to climb aboard.

Dawg, Dash and the helicopter gunner provided cover until the others were aboard.

The truckload of terrorists flew through the compound heading their direction, firing their weapons into the air.

"Go!" Dawg yelled.

Dash ran for the helicopter.

As soon Dash was aboard, Dawg turned and darted for the aircraft as the pilot started to lift off.

When he was near, Dawg leaped.

Rucker and Bull grabbed his arms and hauled him into the craft.

"Go!" Rucker yelled.

The pilot lifted the helicopter up into the air and swung to the east, away from the oncoming vehicle full of angry jihadists, firing their weapons up into the sky.

Until they were out of range, Dawg didn't let go

of the breath he'd held since diving into the fuselage.

"Did anyone see who was in the SUV that got away?" Mac asked.

Rucker shook his head. "No. The windows were dark. All we could tell was that there was a driver and a passenger based on heat signatures."

"We got our target," Bull said.

"Yeah, but who got away?"

"Doesn't matter. We did what we were sent to do," Rucker said. "Kalani is dead, and we can go home."

Dawg climbed into a seat and buckled his harness.

Home to Texas sounded good.

He leaned his head back, thankful they hadn't lost anyone and the world was down one badass son of a bitch responsible for destroying the lives of so many children.

He tried not to dwell on the fact that for every terrorist killed, there were always a couple dozen more ready to take his place.

CHAPTER 1

"Does this dress make me look too desperate?" Beth Drennan tugged at the hem of the little red dress that showed far too much of her thighs. "I don't think I can sit or bend over in this." She shook her head. "No, I can't do it. I'll just wear the jeans I was going to wear." She reached for the jeans she'd pulled off minutes earlier when her best friend had brought her into her bedroom and insisted she needed more appealing clothing for the hail and farewell that evening.

"No way." Nora Michaels snatched the jeans away from Beth's grasp. "It's about time you got back out there. You can't keep moping around after your breakup with Dr. Poor-Excuse-for-a-Fiancé Parker."

"He wasn't a poor excuse," Beth argued. "He was focused."

Nora crossed her arms over her chest. "He didn't have you as his primary focus…ever."

Beth's lips pressed together. She couldn't argue with her friend. She'd fallen in love with Dr. Jonathan Parker while working with him at the Fort Hood Army Hospital. He'd been working there as a civilian while attached to the Texas Army National Guard. The man loved his work, relished challenges and volunteered for every deployment he could get assigned to. Even rescheduling their wedding twice to take on another assignment.

"Admit it," Nora said. "You broke the engagement after the second time he deployed voluntarily to Africa. He didn't put you first for anything."

"He can't help it that he feels compelled to save lives." Beth tired not to grimace while she said that. She'd made excuses for him before.

Nora frowned. "Well, he didn't save his life with you."

"He still wants me to marry him." Beth sighed. "I just don't know if I can deal with being second string with his career always being first. I mean, I know we have to go when we're deployed…I signed up for that, too."

"But to voluntarily deploy when your wedding is only a few weeks away…" Nora shook her head. "He didn't deserve you. At the very least, he should've waited to volunteer until you two were married."

That was why Beth had called off their engagement. She'd told Jonathan he wasn't ready to commit, and she didn't want to tie him down.

"It's been over six months since you two split. It's time to wade back out into the dating pool."

Beth frowned. "I'm not sure I like your analogy. Sounds like I'm heading into deep water without any type of floatation device."

"Swim, baby, swim!" Nora dug a pair of shiny silver heels out of the bottom of Beth's closet. "And wear these."

"I'd rather wear flats," Beth grumbled.

"And I'd rather stay home and make love to my man," Nora said. "But it's a hail and farewell party, and we're going to meet new people and say goodbye to those shipping out."

"But it's not our unit. We don't have to go."

"No, but I have to go because my fiancé asked me to go." She set the shoes on the floor and pointed to them. "And you're going because you're my best friend and you need to meet someone new. You're not getting any younger."

"I'm not even thirty yet."

Nora lifted her chin. "But you're getting close. You're turning twenty-eight next month. Women over thirty are more likely to have difficulties getting pregnant."

Beth snorted. "Especially if they don't have a boyfriend, husband or a friend with benefits."

"Even if they do, they could have difficulties. Your eggs could be drying up as we speak."

"Nora, you're a nurse. For heaven's sake, they have drugs and fertility treatments. I'm not worried about getting pregnant right now. I'm focusing on my career."

Nora's brows rose. "Tick-tock, tick-tock."

"Oh, shut up." Beth bent to slip her feet into the killer heels that would have her weeping by the end of the evening. "If I get a blister, I'm blaming you."

With a grin, Nora slung the strap of her purse over her shoulder. "Hopefully, you won't be wearing them long."

"I'm not into one-night stands," Beth grumbled and straightened. "I feel like I should be walking the corners of the red-light district in Austin, not going to a hail and farewell."

"Well, maybe you'll get lucky, and it'll be worth the blister you'll get in those heels." Nora laughed as she stepped through the door of Beth's apartment. "Here's to hoping."

"I told you, I'm not into one-night stands." Beth stepped through her door, turned and checked that the lock was secure behind her. "Even if I meet someone…interesting…I'm not going to sleep with a stranger." When she turned to face Nora, Beth's eighty-something-year-old neighbor was just coming out of her apartment on the first floor.

Beth's cheeks heated. "Good evening, Mrs. Morris." She prayed the woman wasn't wearing her hearing aid.

"If I was your age and still unmarried, I'd be open to a one-night-stand. The older you get, the fewer available men. They die younger than us females, you know." Mrs. Morris winked. "Enjoy the sex while you can."

Nora burst out laughing. "See? It's not just me. Even your neighbors think your dry spell should be over."

The heat in Beth's face burned even hotter, and she sputtered, "Mrs. Morris…"

The older woman waved a hand. "I'm old. Not dead. I know what a good orgasm feels like." Her lips twisted. "Last one I had was a decade ago. But you don't forget."

The image that blossomed in Beth's mind wasn't good. "Uh…thank you, Mrs. Morris." But then, Mrs. Morris had seen a lot more life, and possibly love, than Beth could ever hope to see. Especially at the rate she was going. "It's good to see you, Mrs. Morris."

The older woman laid a hand on Beth's arm. "Honey, you have to grab for the joy. Life is too short to pussyfoot around. I should know. I've lost two husbands. I know what it is to love and to lose."

Beth frowned. "Doesn't that make you afraid to love again?"

"Not at all," said Mrs. Morris. "You remember the old saying, *It is better to have loved and lost than never to have loved at all.*" The older woman's brow furrowed. "Oh, wait. You might be too young to remember that saying." She shrugged. "Anyway, enjoy your night out. And don't be afraid to fall in love at first sight. I fell in love at first sight with my first husband. We were married for forty years before he died of a stroke. He could be an ornery old cuss, but he knew how to push all my buttons." She heaved a big sigh. "I loved that man." She let go of Beth's arm. "Now, go. You have a lot of living to do before you get to be my age."

Beth followed Nora out to Nora's car.

Nora slid into the driver's seat, grinning from ear to ear.

Beth sat in the passenger seat and pulled the seatbelt over her lap.

Once both doors were closed, Nora burst out laughing. "I like your neighbor."

Her neighbor got into a boat of an old car and settled into the driver's seat, barely able to see over the steering wheel. She smiled and waved at Beth and Nora as she backed out of her parking space.

"Mrs. Morris is one of a kind," Beth said as she waved back.

"And she makes good points," Nora said, wiping tears from her eyes. "You have to live."

"Good grief." Beth flung her hands in the air. "Can't I just go have drinks with a friend without her trying to set me up with another man?"

"I promise not to set you up." Nora shifted into reverse and left the parking lot of Beth's apartment building. "I won't have to. It will likely be at least two to one, men to women, at this hail and farewell. You're an attractive woman. The guys will figure it out without my help." She grinned as she drove to the Salty Dog Saloon outside the main gate of Fort Hood.

Beth cringed. She'd avoided social gatherings involving single, hot-blooded Delta Force men for a reason. They were too…dangerous…and appealed to the daring woman inside of her that she fought to subdue. Working with the special forces men in theater was hard enough. At least while deployed, they had strict orders not to fraternize. Since Nora had fallen for one of the Deltas, Beth preferred to stay home rather than go out with the couple where she was the third wheel. Nora had tried on several occasions to get her to agree to a blind date.

One of the reasons she'd agreed to marry Jonathan was because he wasn't special forces. He was a doctor, someone who worked behind the lines, saving lives, not taking them. A doctor seemed a safe choice. But Jonathan didn't choose safe. He chose to put himself in danger with the assignments he undertook in remote locations where he didn't always have the benefit of being behind the wire in a hardened position.

And he volunteered as often as assignments came up.

Beth had been deployed on a couple rotations to Afghanistan. She'd gone as a volunteer on both rotations. But she hadn't volunteered around the upcoming date of her wedding. Jonathan had, choosing his work over starting their lives together.

After calling off their wedding, Beth had canceled the venue and reception hall and forfeited half of the money she'd paid for flowers, the caterer and the photographer. She couldn't return her dress. Nora, her only bridesmaid, couldn't return her bridesmaid dress. They'd had to eat those costs.

Six months had passed since she'd returned Jonathan's ring. He'd tried several times to get her to reconsider. Those attempts had been from remote locations or while he'd been in transit to his next voluntary assignment, cementing her decision. She'd begun to wonder if she'd been more in love with the idea of being married and starting a life as a married woman than she'd been in love with Jonathan.

With a sigh, she sat forward in her seat as her friend pulled the car into the parking lot of the Salty Dog Saloon and parked. Already, the parking lot was almost full, with more arriving even as Nora and Beth got out of her car.

Beth tugged the hem of her short dress downward, hoping she wasn't flashing anyone a view of the black lace, thong panties she wore beneath. She frowned as she noted other women entering the bar wearing jeans. "I should've worn, jeans," she muttered.

"But you look great in that dress. All the guys will be panting after you."

"I don't want to have men drooling on me like dogs," Beth argued.

"Okay, so maybe not drooling, but they'll be interested." Nora shook her head. "At least, smile. You look like you want to bite someone's head off."

"Good."

Nora stopped and gripped Beth's arm. "Sweetie, I care about you and want you to be happy."

"Then stop pushing me toward every available man." Beth loved that Nora wanted her to be as happy as she was. Beth sighed. "Maybe I'm not ready to let go of Jonathan. Maybe I'm not ready to be happy."

"Six months is a long time to mope, honey." Nora squeezed her arms. "Look, I won't push anyone in your direction if you promise to at least be open to a conversation if someone comes up to you."

Beth stared into her friend's hopeful face. "Okay. I'll try to be open to a conversation, but don't expect me to go home with anyone."

Nora grinned and dropped her hands from Beth's arms. "I won't. We'll take baby steps. That's all I'm asking."

Beth tugged at her dress once more and nodded. "Let's do this. But I'm not staying past ten o'clock. And you might want to give me your keys if you plan on going home with your man."

"Oh, I will be going home with Rucker, but he's riding in with Dash. Rucker's truck is in the shop. We'll drop you off on the way."

Beth stopped in her tracks, nearly tipping over on the impossibly high heels. "You're telling me now? I could've driven my own car."

"You would've chickened out. The only way I could get you to come was to drive you here myself." Nora crossed her arms over her chest and gave her a challenging look. "I'm right, aren't I?"

Her lips pressing tightly together, Beth wanted to tell her friend no, but Nora was correct. If she hadn't insisted on driving, Beth wouldn't be at the Salty Dog Saloon for the little social gathering of the Deltas. She'd have wimped out before she'd even left her apartment.

"I can catch an Uber ride back to my apartment." Beth had brought her cellphone. That was all she needed to call for a ride back to her apartment. "No need for you to drop me off. It would be too far out of your way."

Nora's brow furrowed. "You're not riding with a stranger. Don't worry. We'll get you back to your place."

Yeah, but at what time? Beth squared her shoulders. "Fine. Let's get this over with."

"That's the attitude." Nora rolled her eyes. "You're putting up walls before we even get inside."

Beth tightened her lips. "Just be glad I'm here." She hooked her arm through Nora's and walked through the door into the saloon, where she was immediately bombarded by the noise of people trying to talk over each other and the music.

The introvert in Beth winced.

"Oh, there's Rucker." Nora smiled and waved at her fiancé.

He held up one of the two drinks he had in each hand, indicating he'd already gotten her a drink.

"Go on," Beth said. "I want to get a drink at the bar and find a quiet corner."

Nora raised an eyebrow. "Good luck with that. This place is hopping." She hurried through the crowd to her fiancé.

The tall, dark man engulfed her in an embrace and kissed her soundly before he let go of her.

Longing welled in Beth's chest. Why couldn't

she find that kind of love? Jonathan had always held her at arm's length in public, saving any displays of affection for when they were alone. But he'd been a gentle lover and had made sure she was satisfied…when they were together.

Beth turned to the bartender. "Hey, Sarge," she greeted the bartender and owner of the Salty Dog Saloon, Jim Walker, with a smile.

"Ms. Drennan, it's been a while since you were here. What can I get you?" He tipped his head. "Wait, let me guess…margarita on the rocks."

She smiled. "Not tonight. I'd like a light beer; whatever you have on tap." Margaritas were for when she was in the mood to laugh and have fun. At the moment, she wasn't in the mood for either.

"No margarita?" he said with a dip in his brow. "What's wrong?"

Beth frowned. "Does anything have to be wrong for me to want a beer instead of a marg?"

Sarge chuckled. "No." He filled a mug from the tap and set it on the counter in front of her. "Just different. You've never ordered a beer before."

She sighed, curled her fingers around the handle of the mug and lifted it to take a sip. Foam coated her upper lip. Beth licked it off. "I'm just in a funky mood. I really don't want to be here, but my friend insisted." She looked around for a quiet table. Unfortunately, all the tables had people sitting at them.

Sarge tipped his head toward the empty stool at the far side of the bar. "If you're looking for escape, that seat at the end of the bar is out of the way and as secluded as you can get in a crowded room."

She gave Sarge a weak smile. "Thanks. I just don't want to be bothered.

"Well, you came to the wrong place for that. A lone female in a bar filled with horny men…" Sarge shook his head. "You're doomed before you start."

"I believe you."

Drink in hand, Beth glanced one more time at her friend, Nora, who was happily chatting with a group of young Deltas. She wouldn't miss Beth for a while. Beth dipped her head toward Sarge, walked around a few men seated at the bar and found the only empty stool at the very end. She slid onto the wooden stool and set her beer on the counter, avoiding eye-contact with the man beside her.

Surely, if she didn't acknowledge his presence, he wouldn't try to strike up a conversation.

Out of the corner of her eye, she studied the man. Like the other Deltas present, he was tall, broad-shouldered and damned good-looking. He would have been tempting, had she not sworn off men.

The man lifted his chin toward Sarge. "Can I get another?"

"You bet." Sarge poured whiskey over ice cubes and set the full glass in front of the man.

Beth had seen this man before, on a number of occasions when she'd attended functions with Nora and her fiancé, Rucker Sloan. Beth had met most of Rucker's team, but she couldn't remember all their names. The guy beside her had been at the last barbecue she'd gone to with Nora. Beth hadn't spoken two words to him.

She peeked again under her lashes. If she recalled correctly, this guy's call sign was Dawg.

The man took the drink Sarge handed him and raised it toward Beth. "Here's to finding a quiet corner in a noisy barroom." He tipped his drink back and took a long swallow.

Beth lifted her beer mug, raised it toward him and drank, hoping that would be the end of the conversation, since the man obviously recognized that she'd chosen the corner that was as far away from the crowd as she could get.

Dawg put his drink down and held out his hand. "I'm Doug Masters. You're Beth Drennan, aren't you?"

Well, damn. She wouldn't get the peace and quiet she'd hoped for. Beth set her beer on the counter, sucked in a fortifying breath, took the extended hand and smiled tightly. "I'm Beth. I believe we've met before. They call you Dawg, don't they?"

What would it hurt to talk to him? It would make Nora happy that she was engaging in a conversation with the opposite sex. And It wasn't like she was going home with the guy.

CHAPTER 2

THE MAN'S lips curved into a crooked grin, and he nodded. "Yes, they call me Dawg, for the lack of any other name more interesting. Doug…Dawg… They sound about the same…and I do have a dog. I think I'm one of the few members of our team who does."

Beth tilted her head, strangely open to talking to this stranger who hadn't hit her with a weary pickup line first thing. "What do you do with your dog when you're deployed? Leave him at boarding kennel or a shelter for months at a time?"

He shook his head. "No way. Chewy wouldn't make it in one of those places."

"Is he too aggressive?"

Dawg chuckled. "Yes, but that's not why. He has severe separation anxiety and is afraid of thunderstorms, vehicles backfiring and squirrels burping in the night. I keep a prescription of Xanax on hand at all times."

"What is he, a German Shepherd, pit bull or lab?" Beth asked.

Dawg laughed, his cheeks turning a ruddy red. "Hardly. The little dude only weighs eight pounds. He's some kind of Yorkie, chihuahua mix as far as the vet can guess. He's all black, perky ears and fuzzy with a whole lot of attitude."

Beth grinned. "Not what I pictured you with. How did you come to be the owner of such a small dog?"

Dawg smiled down at his glass of whiskey. "I'm not sure I'm actually his owner. I really think it's the other way around. He owns me."

"How did you find him?"

"I didn't. He found me." Dawg took another sip of his whiskey. "He was wandering around on the street near my house. He ended up making a little den beneath one of the bushes in front of my house and slept there at night. One morning I came out, and this little creature darted out from the bushes. Scared the daylights out of me. I thought he was a rat."

"As small as he was, I'm sure he looked like one," Beth said.

"Yes, he did. But he wasn't eight pounds then. He was only three pounds. All skin, bones and fur. Not much more than a puppy. He was covered in fleas. It took me a week sitting out on the porch in the evening with a bowl of dog food before he'd get close enough for me to reach out and touch him. It took another week before he let me pet him. After that, he moved right in. I treated his fleas, worms and every other parasite that was feasting on his little body. I put him on a diet of healthy food. That little rat ballooned up to eight pounds within a few months. And he sticks to me like glue."

Beth had hoped to be left alone. But after listening to Dawg talk about his little Yorkie mix, she was at ease with the man. He hadn't asked her any questions about herself; he hadn't hit on her or tried to get into her pants. This man really did care for his dog. She found that kind of adorable.

"If he suffers such terrible separation anxiety, what do you do with him when you go out to eat or have to work during the day?"

"He sleeps all day while I'm at work. I have a pet cam set up in my house so I can watch out for him during the day while I'm gone. When I go out at night or when I'm deployed, he stays with my next door neighbor. She feeds him treats and lets him sleep with her at night."

Up to that point, Beth had been enchanted with the big, tough Delta who had a thing for his rescue dog. The mention of another woman gave her pause. "She must be a good friend," Beth said, "to take your dog at the drop of a hat."

Dawg nodded. "She is. And I think she enjoys having Chewy come visit, since she lives alone. She's dog sitting now."

Not that it was any of her business, but Beth had to ask, "Why didn't you bring her with you?"

Dawg's brow wrinkled. "Chewy or my neighbor?"

Beth shrugged, trying to look like she didn't really care, though she did…strangely. "Both or either."

"Chewy gets nervous in crowded environments. Sometimes he gets so nervous, he pees on people."

Beth couldn't help the smile that tilted her lips.

"My neighbor doesn't get out much. At eighty years old, she'd be worn out pretty quickly in a bar. Although I don't think the noise would bother her." He grinned. "She's mostly deaf."

Feeling suddenly happier, Beth smiled. "Being deaf would be an advantage in this place." She sipped the last of her beer before she realized she'd drank the whole mug while Dawg had been talking. She was actually glad Dawg hadn't tried to pick her up.

The man glanced down at his watch and looked around at the folks there for the hail and farewell. "I guess I better make my rounds. I can't keep Mrs. Doherty too late. I want to pick up Chewy." He held out an elbow. "Would you care to make my rounds with me? I'd appreciate an excuse to be leaving earlier than anyone else. The guys give me hell for going home to my dog."

"And how would I be an excuse to leave early?" Beth's eyes rounded. "You want to tell your friends that we're leaving together?"

Dawg gave her a crooked grin. "Come to think of it…" Then he shook his head. "Never mind. My apologies for insulting you. Did you ride with Nora?"

She dipped her head. "I did. But I told her I'd hire a car to get me home."

"So, are you leaving now?"

She smiled and nodded. "I think so. After I make my rounds."

Dawg shook his head. "I take it you didn't really want to come to this shindig."

Beth nodded.

"Is this kind of event not your thing?"

Beth lifted a shoulder and let it fall. "No, it's not that. It's just that she's trying to get me back into the dating scene. I'm just not ready."

Doug winced. "Bad break up?"

She shrugged. "Not really."

"Did he dump you?" Before she could answer his eyes widened. "No, he cheated on you."

"Not really," she said.

His brow furrowed. "How can somebody *not really* cheat on you?"

Beth smiled. "He didn't cheat on me with another woman."

Dawg grinned. "Did he cheat on you with another man?"

"No," Beth said, giving him a mock glare. "He didn't cheat on me. He just chose his career over our relationship."

"Sounds like a Delta." He heaved a heavy sigh. "We have to go when the boss tells us. I guess that means you and me getting together is out of the question."

"No," Beth said.

Dawg grinned. "No, you and me aren't out of the question, or no, he wasn't a Delta?"

She laughed. "No, he didn't leave me high and dry except when he deployed. And I was okay with him deploying. Just not *volunteering* to deploy two weeks before our wedding."

"Curiouser and curiouser," Dawg said with narrowed eyes. "He volunteered? He obviously didn't deserve you."

"It doesn't matter," Beth said. "We broke up months ago."

"But you're still not over him if you're off in a corner thinking about him."

She tilted her head, wondering why she was opening up to this stranger. But she was. "I don't know if it's him I'm not over, or the idea of getting married I'm not getting over. I saw myself getting married before I turned thirty." She raised a hand. "I know…it's old fashioned of me, but I believe in getting married before having children. And I want children some day before I'm too old."

"You have a lot of time left, sweetheart." Dawg frowned. "You're not going to be thirty for another four or five years."

She snorted. "One and a half years. I'll be twenty-nine on my next birthday. I feel my biological clock ticking like a timebomb."

"Sorry," he said. "I didn't mean to pry into your life, and you didn't have to tell me your age." He shook his head. "You're practically ancient."

She swatted at his arm. "You're not helping my ego."

"Sorry, I didn't think women got touchy about their age until they were into their dotage…their forties."

Beth tipped her chin up. "Forty is still young."

"The way you talk, life is practically over after you turn thirty."

"I didn't say I'd get old after thirty. But a woman's most productive years are in her twenties," Beth said.

"And many women have children into their forties," he countered.

"And many women find they can't have children in their thirties. I want them." She grinned. "Now, doesn't that scare you away? A woman who wants to be married, have children and a full, satisfying career?"

He shook his head. "Not at all. I admire a woman who wants it all."

She sighed. "Well, my ex-fiancé didn't admire those attributes enough to stick around for the wedding."

"If you're ready to leave, I'll give you a ride home. Of course, after my rounds of hailing and farewelling." He held up his hands. "No worries. No strings attached. I won't even hit on you... Unless you want me to." He waggled his brows. "I might even invite you to meet my dog. Chewy might have separation anxiety, but he's a lover. He loves everybody. We can share a bowl of water and kibble with him, if you like."

"Now that might be an offer I can't refuse. After your description of Chewy, I think I like your dog more than you at this point."

"Ouch."

"And I do admire a man who isn't afraid to love his dog." Her lips quirked. "All eight pounds of him."

He nodded. "I do love my dog. So, what'll it be?"

"Thank you. I'd love a ride home. And I might like the idea of using the excuse of leaving with you to get me out of staying here until Nora's ready to go. I wasn't too happy about calling on a stranger to give me a ride home."

"If you need someone to vouch for me, you can ask Rucker, Nora's fiancé, about the nature of my character. We go back a long way."

"Strangely enough, I trust you." She slipped her hand through his arm and let him lead her across the floor to the group Deltas and the women who belonged with some of them.

Dawg shook hands with a man Beth hadn't met before and congratulated him on his separation from the military. "Mustang, what's this I hear you're going to work for that security group out of Montana?"

Mustang nodded. "I met Navy SEAL, Hank Patterson, in Afghanistan when the Deltas and the SEALs had a joint mission to take care of some bad guys. He heard I was getting out and contacted me."

"Nice to know you have work in the civilian sector. At least you won't have to pound the pavement looking for a job." Dawg patted the man's shoulder. "And keep me in mind for when my time comes to leave the military."

Mustang nodded. "I'll let Hank know you're interested."

"Thanks."

Beth smiled at Mustang and congratulated him before moving on to other members of Dawg's team, including Rucker.

Nora raised an eyebrow and stared pointedly at Beth's hand curled around Dawg's elbow.

Dawg stepped back and waved a hand toward Beth. "You all know Beth, Nora's friend."

The men nodded, and the women smiled.

"She helped out at the last barbecue we had at Rucker's place," one of the women said. She held out her hand. "I'm Sophie," she said. "When I'm not hanging out with Blade," she patted the man's arm she was leaning on, "I'm working here with Sarge."

"I remember you," Beth said with a smile and took the woman's hand, giving it a firm shake.

"I want the name of the spice you put on the kabobs," Sophie said. "They were so good."

Beth grinned. "I'll text you the name of it when I get back to my apartment." She spoke to a few others of the women while Dawg talked and joked with his friends.

"Well, I hate to break up the party," Dawg said at last. "I need to get home to my dog."

Rucker shook his head. "I thought you found a dog sitter for Chewy."

Dawg nodded. "I did. But she likes to go to bed by nine o'clock."

"Are you leaving too?" Nora asked Beth.

Beth nodded. "Dawg offered to drop me off at my place."

Nora frowned. "Are you sure you don't want to stay?"

"No," Beth smiled. "I'm tired."

Nora's gaze shot from Beth to Dawg and back, a

smile curling her lips. "Well, enjoy the ride and don't do anything I wouldn't do."

Beth's cheeks heated. She wanted to say she wasn't planning on doing anything but didn't want to draw any more attention to herself and Dawg as they left. It wasn't like she was going home with Dawg. He would drop her off at her place and that would be the end of the evening, unless she decided to meet his dog.

Nora hugged her close and whispered, "Dawg's a good guy."

Beth whispered back, "I'm going home…alone."

"Uh-huh." Nora grinned and stepped back into Rucker's arms. "Just have fun."

Dawg held out his hand.

Beth placed hers in his and a little jolt of electricity rippled up her arm and spread throughout her body.

They left the Salty Dog Saloon together.

Despite her determination to remain unfazed by Nora's suggestive glances and words, Beth couldn't help a little shiver of something she hadn't felt in a long time. Desire.

And she'd barely even thought about her ex-fiancé all evening. What did that mean?

It meant the night held all kinds of possibilities. Too bad he was taking her home first.

. . .

DAWG LED Beth across the parking lot to his four-wheel-drive pickup and held the door for her while she climbed up the running board and into the passenger seat. Once she was seated and had secured her belt, he rounded the front of the truck, feeling lighter on his feet than he had in a long time. He suspected it was because of the woman he was taking home...to her apartment.

She wasn't like some of the other women who hung out at the Salty Dog Saloon, hoping to snag a Delta and willing to do anything to get one. They didn't know what they were getting into until the Delta shipped out for months at a time, sometimes with little communication to those back home. Those relationships rarely lasted.

Dawg was tired of the games. Beth had been a breath of fresh air. She'd listened when he'd gone on about his dog and had even sounded interested.

"Do you mind if we get Chewy first and get him settled at my house before I take you home?" he asked. "I wasn't kidding when I said my dog sitter goes to bed at nine o'clock."

"Why should I mind? I'm not in a hurry, and I'm glad to leave the noise. Besides, you're doing *me* a favor by taking me home." Beth smiled. "And after all you've told me about your little guy, I'm interested in meeting him."

He grinned. "Good. We'll get Chewy, settle him

in at my house and then I can take you to your place."

"Chewy sounds like quite the character."

Dawg smiled. "Oh, he is. He's like my kid. I hate to be deployed and leave him behind. But it's my job." He sighed. "In fact, we're due to deploy three days from now. We haven't been back long. I like to spend as much time as I can with Chewy before I leave again. Thankfully, Mrs. Doherty will be here for my guy while I'm gone."

"You're pretty dedicated to the little guy, aren't you?" she said.

"I am. He needed me about the same time as I needed him," Dawg's smile faded. "We lost one of our teammates on a mission. I was feeling pretty low. Having someone to care for helped me stop feeling sorry for myself. I had something else to focus on besides my grief."

"I get that," Beth said quietly. "When my father died suddenly from a heart attack, I was inconsolable. Until my mother took me to get a puppy. Bitty helped me through that time. She was a good little dog."

"What kind?" he asked.

Beth shrugged. "Poodle and something else. Mostly poodle with all her curly dark hair. We got her from a shelter. Someone had dumped her in a field. Thankfully, she was brought to the shelter soon after, and we found her there. She was with me through high school and came with me to college. Sadly, she passed away during my senior year. I joined the Army shortly after I graduated with my nursing degree." She laughed. "Sorry. I didn't mean to go on about myself."

"No, I'm glad you did. I did all the talking in the bar and didn't let you say much so that I could get to know you." He grinned across at her. "I like that you like dogs. That says a lot about you."

"Like what?"

"That you care about something or someone other than yourself." He reached across the console and took her hand. "Thank you for being you."

She squeezed his hand. "I don't think I'd be riding with you now if not for all your talk about Chewy."

He laughed out loud. "I see how it is. You like my dog more than you like me, and you haven't even met him yet."

Beth chuckled. "All your talk about your dog says a lot about you as a man. You have the ability to care about others, even small stray dogs." Her gaze went to where their hands were joined.

Dawg thought she might pull free of his grasp, but she didn't. Instead, she let him continue to hold her hand as she stared at the road in front of them.

He drove the rest of the way to his house, pulled into the driveway and parked the truck. "I hope Mrs. Doherty didn't give up on me." He came around to her side of the truck and helped her down.

When she was on the ground, he touched a hand to the small of her back, turned her toward the little house beside his, hurried to the front door and rang the doorbell.

The sound of a dog barking made him smile.

Beth smiled too. "I take it that's Chewy."

He nodded as the door opened and a small, white-haired woman who couldn't be even five feet tall opened the door with a dog in her arms.

"Oh, good," she said. "Chewy and I were just about to go to bed."

"I'm sorry I was a little late, Mrs. Doherty," Dawg said. "But I can take that little rat off your hands now."

She hugged Chewy and held the wiggly creature out toward Dawg. "He was a perfect angel."

Dawg cocked an eyebrow. "Chewy? An angel?" He snorted. "What did he get into?"

The old woman cackled. "My crochet yarn. He had it strung out all over the living room while I was making supper in the kitchen." She shook her head. "I have to remember to puppy proof my house before he comes again." Her white eyebrows rose. That's in three days, isn't it?"

Dawg nodded. "Yes. Are you still good for keeping Chewy?"

She nodded. "You bet."

Dawg took Chewy from Mrs. Doherty's arms, leaned in and gave the woman a peck on the cheek. "Thank you for taking care of the kid."

She smiled. "Any time. I'm looking forward to having him for a few weeks."

"Hopefully, that will be all it is for this deployment," Dawg said.

"Don't you worry if it's longer," Mrs. Doherty said. "We'll get along just fine."

"I appreciate that." He hugged Chewy. "It makes me feel better knowing I can leave him with someone I know and who cares about him."

The older woman reached out and patted the dog's head. "Chewy and I are pals. You know I'm always here if you need someone to give him a forever home." She grinned. "For however long that is."

"You're going to live to be more than one hundred years old," Dawg said.

Mrs. Doherty snorted. "Sweetie, I don't know if I want to live that long."

"You might not want to live that long, but I sure would like it if you did."

She reached up and patted his cheek. "You're a good boy, Doug."

He smiled. "Thank you. It's nice to know someone cares."

Mrs. Doherty yawned, covering her mouth. "Oh, my. Excuse me. My bed is calling. I'm not as young as you two are." She reached out a hand to Beth. "And by the way, I'm Ruth Doherty. And you are?"

Beth chuckled. "I'm Beth Drennan. Dawg is giving me a ride home."

The older woman squeezed Beth's hand. "He's nice like that. I'd throw my hat in the ring for him if I was a few years younger." She winked.

Dawg winced, his cheeks heating. "Good night, Mrs. Doherty."

"It was nice to meet you," Beth added.

"You too, dear," the older woman said. "And, please, be nice to my neighbor. He's a good guy. You can't go wrong with the boy." She stepped backward into her house, smiled, waved and closed the door between them.

Dawg cupped Beth's elbow and led her across the grass to his house. He pulled the keys from his pocket, inserted it into the door lock, turned the handle and opened the door.

Dawg switched on the living room light.

Chewy immediately wiggled so much that Dawg nearly dropped him.

Dawg set the Yorkie-chihuahua mix on the floor.

Chew scurried away, heading straight for the kitchen and his food bowl.

"He thinks every time his bowl is empty he's going to starve to death."

Beth chuckled. "A justifiable fear, considering where he came from." She stepped through the door ahead of him.

Dawg closed the door behind him. "I'll only be a minute. I need to fill Chewy's food bowl and make sure he has plenty of water. "I know I'll only be gone for a few minutes, but an empty bowl only adds to his separation anxiety."

Beth smiled. "By all means, take care of you dog. I can wait. I'm not in a hurry."

"Can I get you something to drink while you're waiting. Coffee, tea a beer?"

She laughed. "No beer, please. Actually, a cup of hot tea would be nice. I'm surprised you keep tea on hand."

He shrugged. "I never used to be a tea drinker until I deployed a few times and drank tea with the locals in country. I found it to be very calming."

Beth nodded. "Me, too."

"I'll put the pot on stove. You can have a seat at the table..." When she continued to wander around his living room, his lips pressed together. "Or not."

His kitchen, living and dining room was open concept.

As Dawg filled the teapot full of water, his gaze followed Beth's movements as she walked around his furniture. He set the pot on the stove.

Being a bachelor, Dawg wasn't much into fine home décor or room makeovers. What he had purchased for his house was purely functional. Couch, a coffee table he used as his dining table, a television propped up on concrete blocks and two-by-six planks of white pine. The only splash of color in the room was a crocheted pillow on one corner of the couch.

When Beth's gaze landed on it, she turned and grinned. "Mrs. Doherty?"

Dawg nodded. "It was a Christmas gift."

"It's lovely," Beth said.

"Thank you," Dawg said. "I'm kind of partial to it. So far, Chewy hasn't chewed it up. He wasn't quite as much of a puppy as I thought he was. I got him plenty of rawhide to chew on when he went through the baseboard chewing phase. He's really a good little dog, other than the tendency to bark a lot."

The dog in question stood beside his food bowl, looking up at Dawg expectantly.

"I know," Dawg said. "I'm getting food." He reached beneath the counter below the sink, pulled out a bag of dog food and shook some into the bowl. Dawg pulled a carton of chicken broth out of the refrigerator and poured it over the dog food.

Chewy sniffed the contents of the bowl, ate a couple of bites then crawled into is fuzzy dog bed.

Dawg glanced across to where she stood in the living room, a smile on her face.

"See?" Doug lifted his hands, palms upward. "It's not that he's hungry."

"In this case, he's not anxious. He's food insecure,"

With a smile, Dawg tipped his head toward Chewy's bowl. "He deserves to get the royal treatment."

"He's a lucky dog now that he has you."

"And with Mrs. Doherty as backup," Dawg added. "I'm fortunate to have her as a neighbor."

"Yes, you are," Beth said with a smile. "It's like she's Chewy's grandmother."

Dawg grinned. "That's exactly how I feel. But then I feel like she's my grandmother as well."

Beth's smile broadened. "She's old enough to be."

"Yes," Dawg said. "But I don't tell her that. It might hurt her feelings. Besides, you heard her… she's sweet on me."

"Yes, she is," Beth said. "And she wants you to be happy. She warned me to be nice to you."

Dawg's eyes widened. "She did?"

Beth nodded. "Does she say that to all the ladies you bring home?"

He shook his head. "I've never taken a woman to meet Mrs. Doherty. In fact, I don't bring women to my house. You're the only one I've brought to meet her."

"Should I feel honored?" Beth asked.

"Absolutely," he said.

"And I got to see the infinitely entertaining Chewy."

Upon hearing his name, Chewy got up out of his bed and trotted over to where Beth stood in the living room, as if remembering he hadn't greeted her properly.

Beth kneeled down, pulling the skirt of her short dress down over her thigh. "That's right. I got to meet this handsome boy." She ruffled the dog's ears.

Chewy leaned into her fingers and tipped his head up, closing his eyes as if in ecstasy.

"Told you he was a lover." Dawg's pulse climbed at the expanse of skin exposed. He gulped and glanced away. Beth made a pretty picture, smiling and petting his dog, but he couldn't watch without feeling a little jealous of the attention she was giving the mixed-breed mutt.

"I think he likes me," Beth said.

"Yes, you've scored points with him. He loves having his ears scratched. He probably has memories of when I found him. He had ear mites. The other parasites I had the vet treat him for." Dawg held up his hands. "It's okay. He doesn't have them anymore. He just loves having his ears scratched."

"He appears well taken care of. I don't mind scratching his ears. The dog I grew up with loved having her ears scratched." She straightened and entered the kitchen.

Chewy trotted along behind her. When she stopped, he stopped.

"What can I do to help?" she asked.

He smiled and looked down at the dog behind her. "You have a friend."

"Best kind of friend there is," she said with a smile. "I'd get a dog, but I'm kind of afraid to. I live in an apartment, and I don't have the neighbor you have, who would gladly dog sit for me when I'm deployed. Besides, being in an apartment isn't fair to a dog. He'd need a yard to run and play in."

"That's part of the reason I have a house instead of downsizing to an apartment. I really think I was meant to have Chewy. A friend of mine sold me this place. It was a fixer upper. He'd started the work, but was transferred to another post. He needed to find someone who could recognize that it had good bones and someone who had the skills and commitment to see it through completion."

"And that person was you? Were you always skilled at carpentry?" Beth asked.

"I worked one summer as a carpenter's assistant on a couple of building sites. I learned enough to get by. Everything else I looked up on the internet." He grinned. "You can find just about any do-it-yourself project on video. Thankfully, the electricity and plumbing had already been done. I refinished the wood floors to their original glory. The bathrooms got all new fixtures and tile, and I replaced all the windows with double-pane windows."

Beth shook her head. "Sounds like it cost a fortune."

"The supplies cost, but the labor was free. I have a lot of sweat equity in the place. I painted the inside and the outside."

Beth nodded toward the walls of the living room. "I like the color. It's neutral. Anything can go in this room."

Dawg laughed. "You should have seen the colors in here before I started. The place had been built in the seventies. Everything was still in the original color palette…avocado greens and golds. The carpet hiding the wooden floors was a threadbare burnt orange shag."

Beth winced. "Yikes."

"I tore out the cabinets in the kitchen and those overhanging the bar, making it more open-concept. I had granite counters installed and did the tilework on the backsplash myself." He waved a hand toward the kitchen wall.

"It's all so nice, crisp and clean. Like a whole new house," Beth commented. "Not many people would take on such a huge project."

He shrugged. "I did it in between deployments over the past year and a half. Chewy got used to all the noise and could sleep through almost anything...as long as I was still there. My pride and joy is the deck I built out back. Now, I enjoy sitting outside under an umbrella while Chewy plays in the yard. The furniture I get the most use out of is the table and chair set on the deck. That, and the umbrella makes sitting outside under the hot Texas sun bearable." He stared out the back window beyond the living room. "If I was here more often, I'd consider putting in a pool. Chewy likes to swim. I've taken him out to the lake several times. He gets right in and paddles around."

The pot on the stove whistled.

Dawg retrieved a couple of mugs from the cabinet and set them on the counter. He placed a tea bag in each and poured steaming water over them. "Cream or sugar?" he asked.

"You have cream?" she asked.

"I do. I like it in my coffee on occasion. Usually, I drink it black as I'm running out the door."

Beth smiled. "I take my tea without sugar or cream. I'm not much of a coffee drinker. I learned to drink it when deployed, as it's easier to find than tea."

"True." Dawg handed her the mug. "Careful. It's hot." He carried his mug to the table, set it down and held a chair for her, scooting it in as she sat.

Beth wrapped her hands around the mug and

stared at the dog now lying in his bed. "Chewy's a special pup."

Dawg nodded. "Yes, he is. I hate that I have to leave him again so soon."

"Do you know where you're going?" Beth asked.

He nodded. "But I can't say where."

"I understand," Beth said.

Dawg found it refreshing to find a woman who knew what it was like to deploy, and the secrecy necessary to keep the team and their mission safe.

She reached across the table for his hand. When he took hers, she said, "I wish you luck."

"Thanks." He squeezed her hand gently. "I don't suppose you'd go out for a cup of tea with me?"

She laughed. "I'm having one now."

He gave her lopsided grin. "Right. But I mean tomorrow. I'd ask you out to dinner, but that might be too much of a commitment for someone trying to avoid a relationship right now."

She nodded. "True…but a girl has to eat, and it would be nice to have company while doing so. Tomorrow night?"

"Yes, ma'am." Dawg nodded. "Unfortunately, I'm on a tight schedule and shipping out soon."

"I can do tomorrow night," she said.

"Great. I can pick you up at six-thirty, if that's all right."

"Sounds good."

Chewy opened an eye, rolled onto his back and closed the eye again.

"We should be going," Dawg said. "I need to get you back to your place so you can get some rest."

"The tea was wonderful," Beth said, sipping once more.

"It's just plain black breakfast tea. Nothing fancy or flavored."

"My kind of tea," Beth said. "I don't like the ones with all the flavors, either."

"There you go," Dawg said. "We have something in common besides our love of dogs."

She took another sip of her tea. "This evening turned out a lot different than I expected."

"Same." Dawg tipped his head toward the sleeping dog. "With the looming deployment, I wanted to spend more time at home with Chewy. You got me out of the hail and farewell early. I'll be spending more time with my team in the near future. I'll have my fill of them."

"What about the guy who was leaving?"

"Mustang's on a different team. But we worked together on several missions."

Beth took one last sip, stood and carried her mug to the sink. "Thanks again for the tea and conversation."

Dawg followed and laid his mug in the sink beside hers. Their shoulders brushed briefly. A shock of electricity ran through his arm and down to his groin. There had been no flirting between them and certainly nothing sexual. Surprisingly, he felt more of a connection with her than any other woman he'd dated in the past few years. He looked forward to taking her out the next evening. He didn't expect it to lead anywhere since he'd deploy shortly afterward. He'd be gone for weeks, maybe months.

When he grabbed his keys from the counter, Chewy popped out of his bed and followed him to the front door. "Stay, Chewy," he said firmly.

The dog looked up at him with those big soulful eyes.

Beth smiled down at the little mixed breed mutt. "I don't mind if he comes with us. He can sit in my lap."

"It's okay," Dawg said. "He'll calm down as soon as we leave." He walked out and held the door for Beth then made sure Chewy didn't sneak out before he closed the door and locked it.

He drove to Beth's apartment complex a couple miles from his home. They talked about Fort Hood, being in the Army and the changes that had occurred in the uniforms since they'd joined. He felt comfortable talking with her, and she seemed equally comfortable with him. Again, a nice change from the civilian women he'd dated before.

When he stopped in front of her apartment complex, she started to get out by herself.

BREAKING TIES

Dawg hurried around and held her door for her as she climbed down from the truck.

"I can make it to my door on my own," she said with a twisted smile.

"I know you can, and you've likely done it a thousand times." He held out his hand. "But I'd feel better if you humored me and let me walk you to your door."

She stared at that hand for a moment, and then took it. "Okay."

When they reached her door, she turned. "Thank you for seeing me safely home. I enjoyed talking with you and meeting your neighbor and dog."

"I'll see you tomorrow around six-thirty?"

She nodded and turned, pushing her key into the lock and opening the door. She started to step inside, hesitated, and then turned back toward him, stood on her tiptoes and brushed a quick kiss across his lips.

Then she entered her apartment and closed the door behind her.

Dawg stared at the closed door for a long moment, a grin spreading across his face. The evening had ended a lot different that he'd expected. And he looked forward to seeing her the next evening.

He returned to his truck, climbed in and drove out of the parking lot. Looking back at the building, he wondered what would have happened if he'd had the opportunity to kiss her back.

That might have pushed her to her limits, and she might have called off their dinner the following night. Perhaps it was better he'd stood in stunned silence while she'd brushed her lips across his.

He could still feel the softness of her lips on his and was glad he'd been persistent in asking her out the following night. The next day couldn't get there soon enough.

His lips curled in a happy smile as he drove back to his house and his little dog.

CHAPTER 3

AFTER BETH HAD CLOSED the door to her apartment, she'd closed the door and leaned against the paneling, wondering what the hell had come over her to kiss the man.

Nothing in their conversation had been that personal. He hadn't come on to her, and she hadn't flirted with him.

Then why had she thought kissing him was acceptable? He might have asked her out to dinner because she hadn't thrown herself at him. And there, at the last, she'd done just that. Thrown herself at him.

Yet he hadn't argued or turned her away. But he had stood there, looking a little shocked at her little display of affection.

Her eyes widened. She hadn't give him her

phone number. Even if he wanted to call off their date, he wouldn't be able to.

For that matter, she didn't have his number. She couldn't chicken out at the last minute and call to cancel. Or could she? If she really wanted to get his number, she could call Nora and have her ask Rucker for Dawg's digits. As far as that went, Dawg could ask Rucker to get her number from Nora.

Beth sighed. She had a date for tomorrow night. A thrill of anticipation raced through her as she pushed away from the door and walked through her apartment, stripping her clothes as she went. When she reached the bathroom, she turned on the shower, adjusted the water temperature and stepped beneath the spray, letting the rivulets run over her head and shoulders. The water slipped over her breasts and down her torso. Images of Dawg joining her in the shower popped into her mind.

What would he be like as a lover? Not that she'd ever find out. Tomorrow's dinner was just a date. Nothing else. There was also the issue of her being an officer while he was enlisted. Fraternizing between officers and enlisted was highly frowned upon. Thankfully, they weren't under the same command. That would make it even worse.

The fact was that she liked him and looked forward to seeing him again.

When Beth turned off the shower, she heard the buzz of her cellphone and smiled, thinking Dawg had gone to the effort of getting Rucker and Nora to give him her number.

Hurriedly, she wrapped a towel around her body and ran into the kitchen where she'd left her cellphone in her purse. With a smile on her face, she fished the device out of the depths of her purse and looked down at the caller ID. Beth frowned. It wasn't Dawg. Instead, it was her commanding officer.

Got a mission for you. Can you be ready to bug out in forty-eight hours?

Beth's pulse raced. She'd never been deployed in that quick of a timeframe. Truthfully, she didn't have anything holding her back, like a dog or children. She didn't have a spouse to answer to, and the staff at the hospital would cover for her in her absence.

There was the dinner tomorrow night. She could make that if her pre-deployment preparations didn't take all day and night.

With a sigh, she texted back.

Can do.

Her commander responded

See you at the office 0600.

Beth snorted. So much for a good night's sleep. But then she could sleep on the airplane to wherever she was going. In the meantime, she went through her go bag, her closet and her laundry to make sure she had what she might need on a deployment. She went through her uniforms, unpacked and repacked her go bag.

Forty-eight hours wasn't much time to prepare, especially if she had a lengthy mission briefing to attend, medical screening or vaccinations that might be required before being shipped out.

It was after midnight when she finally laid down in her bed and stared up at the ceiling, thinking about Dawg. She might still have to get Nora to have Rucker give her Dawg's number. If the briefings went long into the next night, she might have to call off their dinner. She hoped they wouldn't, and that she would get to see the man before she departed. It would be nice to have one last good meal before she was shipped off to who knew where.

It would be a good send off for her, and for him, since he was being deployed as well.

She lay awake for a long time, going over their conversation of the evening. She'd thought very little about Jonathan. And now that she was alone in her apartment, all she could think about was how she'd kissed Dawg and how she wanted to kiss him again. Only a real kiss this time.

They had one night together before they each

deployed. After that, it could be weeks, maybe months before they saw each other again.

Beth vowed to make it a good night.

6:25 PM the next evening...

"I SHOULD HAVE CANCELLED." Beth threw the fifth dress on the bed on top of the others.

"You'll be fine," Nora said. "How about this one?" She held up a little black dress. "It's perfect. You can dress it up or down with shoes and accessories."

"I don't even know where he's taking me. We could be going to a brewery, in which case, jeans and a T-shirt might be the right thing to wear."

"You can never go wrong with a little black dress. The key is to wear it like you mean it." Nora held the dress up in front of her. "You have four minutes to get dressed. I suggest you make up your mind."

Beth grabbed the dress, yanked it off the hanger and slipped it over her head. She spun around. "Zip me?"

Nora laughed. "For someone who can be so organized and put together on the hospital floor, you're a complete disaster with relationships."

"I can't help it. I feel like I have no control over what happens. And you know how nutty that makes me feel."

Nora nodded. "I get it. Relationships can be difficult at their best and impossible at their worst. But Dawg's a good guy. He won't do anything to hurt you."

"I didn't think Jonathan would, either." She stared at herself in the mirror as Nora pulled the tab up on the back, zipping her into the form-fitting dress. It fit her like a second skin. The fabric stretched and moved without making her feel trapped inside. "It'll have to do," she muttered.

A knock sounded on the door to her apartment.

Nora shoved a pair of heels into her hands. "Hurry up. He's here. Want me to get the door?"

Beth shook her head. "No. I'll get it."

"Okay, then I'll hide out in here until after you two leave." She hugged Beth. "Relax. You'll be fine. And you have on your sexy underwear in case it gets interesting." She winked. "Have fun."

"I'll be fine?" she whispered. "I'm shaking like a leaf!"

"Go, before he thinks you stood him up." Nora turned her around and gave her gentle push toward the door.

Beth crossed the living room floor, still holding the heels in her hands.

Another knock made her jump.

She peeked through the peephole.

"Really?" Nora snorted. "Who else would it be?"

"Shh," Beth hissed. "A girl can't be too careful." The man on the other side of the peephole was the one who'd promised to pick her up at six-thirty. And he was handsome, sexy and made her knees weak.

What was she thinking going out on a date with him? She wasn't ready.

But then she was heading out on deployment in twenty-four hours. What did she have to lose? She'd have weeks to regret the night, or weeks of remembering how wonderful it was. If she didn't go, she'd wonder which it would have been.

Beth sucked in a deep breath and opened the door.

Dawg had almost given up when Beth's door swung open.

She stood there in a little black dress, holding her shoes in her hand.

He grinned, his heart soaring at the sight of her standing there, even more beautiful than the night before. "I thought you'd changed your mind."

"I almost did," she admitted.

"But you didn't." He stepped back. "Ready?"

She started through the door.

"Uh," he frowned. "You might want to put on your shoes before we leave."

For a moment, she stared at him as if confused.

"Your shoes?" He nodded to the heels she had dangling from her fingertips.

"Do you like them?" She looked down at her hands and frowned. "Oh. Right." Her cheeks reddened, and she leaned over to slip her feet into the strappy heels. When she had them on, she glanced up. "I'm ready now."

When he held out his hand, she placed hers in his.

It was warm, unlike so many other women whose hands he'd held. He liked that about her. And he liked her smile and the way she wore dresses and did her hair. Hell, he liked everything about her.

"All day long, I've been looking forward to tonight." He pulled her hand through the crook of his arm. "I hope you like Italian food."

"I do," she said.

"Anything in particular?" he asked.

"Just about everything." Beth laughed. "I haven't met an Italian dish I didn't like."

"Then I hope you like chicken parmesan."

"One of my favorites," she said.

"Perfect," he patted her hand on his arm and waited while she pulled her door closed behind her.

For a moment, he thought he saw someone else inside her apartment, but the door closed too soon for him to be certain.

"Where are you taking me?" Beth asked.

His shoulders pushed back, and he lifted his chin. "To a place that makes the best chicken parmesan around."

"And where might that be?"

"My place."

She frowned. "Your place?"

"If you don't mind a homecooked meal… If you had your heart set on going to a restaurant, we can do that instead. I don't want you to be uncomfortable." He stood in front of her apartment. "I just thought it would be nice to have homecooked one more time before I deployed, and I'd get to share my time with you and with my dog."

Beth shook her head. "Stop."

He lifted his hand and cupped her cheek. "Please don't say you've changed your mind."

She covered his hand with hers. "Not at all. In fact, I'd prefer a homecooked meal. I don't cook often enough, and I got word last night that I'm deploying, too. The thought of months of MREs or mess hall food makes my stomach churn. I'd love a homecooked meal I don't have to make."

Dawg blew out a breath. "Thank goodness. If you hadn't wanted to eat it, I'd have had to give it away or put it out with the trash."

"Oh, please." Beth looked at him in horror. "Don't waste it. I love chicken parmesan." She took his arm again. "Lead the way. I'm practically drooling."

He laughed and walked with her to his truck. "You had me worried for a moment."

"I had myself worried. I wasn't sure I was ready for a real date after breaking my engagement. But when I got the news I was shipping out soon, I thought…" she shrugged, "why the hell not?"

"I should be glad you got orders?" He chuckled and then frowned. "I'm not so sure. Do you know where you're going?"

She shook her head. "Not yet. I get my briefing in the morning and fly out tomorrow night."

"Wow. And I thought our missions were secretive." He covered her hand with his. "I hope they aren't sending you somewhere terribly dangerous."

"You and me both. But it's a gig I signed up for. I get orders, I go."

"How often have you deployed?"

"I've only gone once before to Afghanistan." She climbed into the passenger seat of his truck.

Dawg rounded the front of the truck and got in. "That's right. We were there at the same time as you and Nora. That's when Rucker met Nora."

Beth nodded. "They did meet there. Funny how small the world is."

"Especially in the Army," he agreed.

The drive to his house was accomplished quickly.

When they rolled into his driveway, he shifted into park, cut the engine and got out, his pulse hammering as soon as his feet hit the ground. He had Beth at his house where he could charm her with his culinary skills and his cute dog. He didn't dare to hope it would lead to more than good conversation and maybe...just maybe...another kiss.

He wouldn't mind if the evening culminated in more than a kiss, but he wouldn't rush her. She deserved better treatment than that.

Dawg hurried around to open the truck door for her and helped her down and into his arms.

It felt natural. For a moment, he held her there, and then stepped back. "Sorry. I couldn't help myself."

"No worries," she murmured, her cheeks flushing a pretty pink.

"Chewy will be happy to see you. I thought about having Mrs. Doherty watch him tonight, but I couldn't. I'm going to miss him a lot while I'm gone."

"I'm glad he's here," Beth said. "He's good company.

Dawg unlocked the front door and waved a hand for Beth to enter.

Chewy was there to greet her, jumping up against her legs.

She bent to scratch his ears and sweep a hand across his back. "How's my little guy?" she murmured.

"If you two can entertain yourselves, I want to put the noodles on the stove. The chicken is in the oven warming. I finished cooking it before I came to get you."

She straightened, smiling. "You really did put a lot of thought and effort into this meal, didn't you?"

He lifted a shoulder and let it drop. "I like to cook, especially when the food is appreciated. If you'd told me you didn't like Italian, we'd have gone out to eat, and I wouldn't have mentioned the chicken parmesan."

"In that case, I'm so glad I told you I liked Italian."

"Give me a few minutes," he said. "I'll have it all on the table."

"Let me help."

"I'd appreciate it." He led the way. "It's just the last-minute things."

Beth followed him into the kitchen.

Dawg turned on a gas burner beneath the pot of water he'd set out for cooking the noodles. "If you want to get the salad out of the refrigerator, you can set it on the table." He pulled a long baguette out of a plastic wrapper, laid it on a cutting board and started slicing.

Beth retrieved the bowl of salad from the refrigerator and placed it on the table. When she returned, she found a stick of butter in the fridge and set it on the counter beside the bread. "Want me to slice, butter and sprinkle garlic salt on the bread?"

He stopped halfway through and handed her the serrated knife he'd been using. "For the record, you don't have to help. I invited you out to dinner, not to cook dinner."

"For the record…" she said with a cocked eyebrow, "I don't mind. I like feeling useful."

While he poured noodles into boiling water, she sliced the bread, then added butter and garlic.

Fifteen minutes later the noodles were ready, and the garlic bread was toasted. They each filled their plates with spaghetti noodles, marinara, chicken parmesan and garlic bread and carried them to the table.

Dawg opened a bottle of merlot and poured it into two wine glasses. "I had to buy these today. I don't need goblets for beer."

Beth laughed. "This is very much a bachelor's pad." She lifted her wine glass. "To you, for providing the wine and the glass to drink it in." She lifted her glass to him. "And thank you for a last home-cooked meal before I have to leave."

He held his glass up to her. "To you, for giving me your last night before deploying and for being flexible on where we'd go to eat."

They sipped the wine then took their seats.

Chewy curled up on his bed nearby and snoozed while Beth and Dawg talked over their dinner.

Dawg couldn't remember laughing so much or enjoying someone else's company as much.

Beth seemed to enjoy it as well, chuckling at his jokes and sharing stories about some of her patients during deployment. When they were done eating, they sat longer, talking about anything and everything or nothing at all.

Beth helped him clean the table and the dishes, rinsing them off to place them in the dishwasher. They bumped shoulders often, making Dawg hyper-aware of her in that little black dress.

When they were done, he hung the dishtowel on the oven door. "Let me make you a cup of tea. Or would you prefer more wine?"

"Tea, please," she said.

He reached for the tea kettle, filled it with water and set it on the stove.

"Where are the mugs?" she asked.

"I'll get them. You can have a seat in the living room."

She nodded. "Good. I want to get out of these shoes. They're killing me." Beth bent to slip the straps off the back of her heels and stepped out of the high heels. "They're pretty but not practical."

"Get comfortable," he said. "I'll be right in."

A few minutes later, he carried the mugs of tea into the living room and set one down on the coffee table, the other in her hand. "Careful, it's hot."

He settled on the sofa beside her, placed his mug on the coffee table, kicked off his shoes and settled back. "I doubt we'll have air conditioning where we're going. I have to enjoy it while I can." He leaned back his head on the cushion and closed his eyes.

Peeking between his eyelids, he studied Beth with her sandy-blond hair and blue eyes.

She laid her tea on the table, leaned back beside Dawg and reached for his hand.

Dawg gladly held her hand as they lounged together on the couch for a few long minutes. He didn't dare make any advances. If she wanted more, she'd have to make the first move.

Hell, Dawg prayed she would, because his body was already on fire and burning to take her into his arms. They sat so closely together…yet too far apart, and he wasn't quite sure how to bridge the gap, or if she'd be receptive to doing so.

For several minutes, Beth lay against the couch cushion, her eyes closed.

After a while, he whispered, "Are you asleep?"

She chuckled without opening her eyes. "No. I'm debating getting up to leave or snuggling with you here on the sofa. But it's been too long since I've been on a date, and I just feel...awkward." She turned her head toward him, stared into his eyes and gave him a crooked grin.

"Let me help you decide." He slid an arm behind her neck and pulled her into his arms. "Better?" he whispered into her ear.

"Mmm. Much." She turned a little on her side and laid her cheek against his chest. "I like this."

He sighed and tightened his arm around her shoulders. "Me, too."

"Is it just because we're both about to deploy, and we're clinging to the comforts of home that we're feeling the need for contact with another human?"

He laughed. "Comfort is not what I'm clinging to right now," he said. "Excitement? Yes. Comfort? No way."

She leaned her head back and frowned. "Excitement?"

"Sweetheart, I've been dying to spend time with you since that last barbecue, but you didn't even know I was alive."

"I do now," she said softly, her hand curling into his T-shirt. "I was too focused on not making eye contact with any of the eligible men at that event...

like the hail and farewell. I didn't think I was ready to jump back into the dating pool."

"And now?" he said softly.

"I'm still not jumping back in," she assured him. "Somehow, I don't think going out with you is the same thing."

"Because you don't see me as date material?" he asked, his chest tightening.

"No. Because you don't make me feel like a teen on her first date. You make me feel—"

Dawg stiffened. "If you say comfortable, we're calling it a night, and I'm taking you home."

Her chuckled warmed his chest. "No, not comfortable…but like I've come home to a very nice place. A place that stirs my heart and my blood. I don't feel like I have to jump through hoops to impress you."

"You don't," he said. "Well, maybe just one hoop might be fun." He held up his hand. "Just kidding. I should be jumping through hoops for you."

"You did. You made dinner for us." Her grin spread across her face. "And it was amazing." She tipped her head up. "Thank you." She leaned close and pressed her lips against his.

Dawg didn't miss this opportunity. Not this time. He tightened his hold around her and crushed his lips against hers.

When she opened to him, he dove between her teeth and caressed her tongue with his.

Cupping the back of her neck with the palm of his hand, he deepened the kiss, loving the way she tasted of Italian seasoning and garlic.

Her fingers slid across his chest and downward. When she reached the hem of his T-shirt, she shoved it upward and smoothed a hand over his naked chest.

He cover her hand with his, slowing her exploration, his breath hitching in his chest. "Are you sure you want to go this route?"

She nodded. "Yes."

"Once you get my engine revving, I don't know how easy it'll be to shut it down."

Beth laughed. "Really? You're going to use a mechanical analogy?"

He smiled down into her eyes. "What analogy would you rather I use?"

She shrugged. "Maybe an animal reference."

"Like a mouse or platypus?" he teased.

"Don't be silly. More like a lion or tiger."

"Oh, I get it, you want something that could hurt you, like a lobster." He tilted his head. "Once you get my claws snapping, I don't know if I can…" He laughed out loud. "No. I can't do that. It loses any kind of sexiness when you have hard shell claws involved."

She drummed her fingers on his chest. "Go back to the engine analogy."

"As I was saying…" He gathered her closer,

tipped her chin up and bent his head, his lips hovering over hers. "Once you get my engine revved, I'm not sure I can power back. You'll have to be certain this is what you want."

She placed a finger over his lips. "Stop talking and start living."

She didn't have to tell him twice.

CHAPTER 4

BETH ROLLED OVER ONTO HIM, straddling his hips, her knees pressing into the couch cushions. Now that she'd started down this path, she didn't want to stop. "I don't want to miss anything about this night or the possibilities that it holds. I leave tomorrow. I need something to hold me over until I get back."

Dawg rested his hand on her hips. "I have protection, but it's in the bedroom."

Beth drew in a deep breath, threw back her head and let the air out slowly. Then she climbed off his lap, held out her hand and pulled him to his feet. "Last one there has to give the other a back rub." Before he could get off the couch, she was halfway down the hall, giggling as she went.

He caught up with her as she reached his

bedroom door. Dawg scooped her into his arms and carried her the rest of the way into his room and set her on her feet. "Now is your time to back out. If you don't, all bets are off."

"I'm willing to take that wager and raise you one." She pushed his T-shirt up over his head and tossed it against the wall. Then her hands rose to the back of her dress her fingers curling around the zipper tab. She drew it downward, ever so slowly.

Dawg brushed her hands aside and finished lowering the zipper down her back and pushed the straps of the dress off her shoulders.

The fabric slipped over her hips and dropped to the floor. She stood in nothing but a pair of black, lace, thong panties, her breasts naked, exposed to his gaze. Rather than cover them, she pushed her shoulders back and tipped her chin up.

"Beautiful." Dawg groaned and captured her butt cheeks in his hands, lifting her up.

She wrapped her legs around his waist and lowered herself over his hard erection, encased in blue denim jeans.

He groaned again.

Beth liked that he was so hard with his desire for her. It made her feel powerful. She cupped his cheeks between her palms and leaned down to press a kiss to his lips, opening to let in his tongue.

He swept past her teeth, deepening the kiss

until she was breathless and hungry for so much more.

Dawg laid her on the edge of the bed, her legs dangling over the side.

His chest was as broad and muscular as she'd imagined. Several scars added character to the smooth, tanned skin.

Beth's pulse quickened. She sat up and reached for the button on his jeans, pushing it loose. Then she gripped the tab on his zipper and pulled it downward slowly, thinking *boxers or briefs?*

When his cock sprang free, she gasped.

Commando!

She pushed the jeans over his hips and down his legs.

Dawg shoved them the rest of the way down and stepped free. He stood before her naked and stunningly sexy.

Her breath caught and held in her throat as she reached out to cup his erection in her hand.

Slowly, she moved her fingers over his hard length, loving the velvety smoothness over the rock-hard strength of his desire. Tracing the tip of her finger over the head, she bent to touch her tongue to the tip where a drop of moisture glistened.

His body stiffened, and he gripped her hair in his hands.

Slowly, savoring every moment, every taste and texture, Beth closed her mouth over his cock and drew him in.

Dawg threw back his head, his hands tightening in her hair, urging her to take more.

She sheathed him with her lips until he bumped against the back of her throat. For a long moment, she held him there, flicking her tongue around his girth. Then she slid her hands around his backside and urged him out of her and back in, establishing a pace he picked up.

He moved gently in and out of her mouth, careful not to gag her.

Heat coiled around her core, manifesting itself in moisture between her thighs. She wasn't sure how much longer she could wait to have him inside her. Already, she was tingling at her center.

When Dawg pulled out of her, he dropped to his knees in front of her, parting her legs. "Your turn," he said, his voice deep and gravelly as if he were holding onto control by a thread.

"You don't have to," she said and gasped as he parted her folds and flicked her clit with the tip of his tongue.

"Oh, sweet heaven," she moaned and fell back against the comforter, her fingers gripping the fabric, holding on to keep herself grounded while he sent her body to the moon.

Again and again, he flicked her there and nibbled and licked until Beth could barely breathe.

The tension in her body mounted. Every breath she took hitched. She wove her hands into his hair as she shot over the edge, sensations racing through her system with her release.

For a long time, she pulsed, her hips rocking, her head thrown back.

Dawg continued his attack, licking, flicking and stroking her until she fell back to earth, satiated, yet wanting more.

Then he climbed to his feet, reached into the drawer beside the bed and grabbed a small packet.

Beth took it from his fingers, tore it open and rolled the condom down over his shaft.

Dawg bent to claim her lips, tasting of her. As he did, he touched his cock to her drenched entrance and eased into her.

Beth wrapped her legs around his waist.

As he stood beside the bed, Dawg moved in and out of her, picking up speed with every thrust until he rocked like a piston. His hands on her hips, he pounded into her until his body stiffened and he thrust one last time, burying himself deep inside of her.

For a long moment, he held her there, his head back, his eyes closed and his jaw hard. When his cock quit throbbing against her channel, he drew in a long, slow breath and let it out. "Wow," he said and pulled free of her. Then he helped her slide up on the bed and laid down beside her, gathering her into his arms. "Are you really leaving tomorrow?" he whispered against her neck, nuzzling her earlobe.

She nodded. "I report in the morning for my briefing. I have to have my gear with me because we're leaving soon after."

"I'd like to see you again," he said.

She smiled and touched his lips with the tips of her fingers. "I'd like that, too."

His brow furrowed. "Problem is...I don't know when that will be."

She chuckled. "I'll leave an opening on my calendar when I return."

"Seriously." He smoothed a hand over her hair and brushed his thumb along her jawline. "I want to see you a lot more. I wish we had found each other well before being deployed. I feel like we're out of time."

She turned and shot a glance at the clock on the nightstand. "Actually, we are out of time. I need to get back to my place. I still have a few things to pack and I have to be up before the crack of dawn."

"Right," Dawg rolled up on his arm and stared down into her eyes. "You're a beautiful woman, Beth Drennan. I'm glad we were both trying to escape the crowd at the Salty Dog last night."

She smiled up at him. "Me, too. Who knew the

night would only get better? And I got to meet Chewy."

Dawg kissed her, hard, taking her in his arms and holding her close, skin to skin.

When he raised his head, his lips pressed into a flat line. "I need to get you home." He rolled out of the bed, grabbed his jeans and pulled them on. Then he snagged Beth's dress and panties and handed them to her.

She swung her legs out of the bed and stood, beautifully naked and unashamed or shy. She stepped into her dress and pulled it up her body, sliding her arms into the straps. Then she turned for him to zip the back.

He did so, gladly, his knuckles brushing her skin, making him want to take her back to bed.

When he finished, Beth leaned back against his chest. "I wish I didn't have to leave right now."

Dawg swept his hands down her arms to her hips. He leaned close and pressed a kiss to the curve of her neck. "Do you have to?"

"Mmm. Soon," she said and turned in his arms.

His lips curved. "Real soon?" He slid his hands under the hem of her dress and cupped her naked ass.

Her irises flared, and she moved closer, pressing her hips to his. "Maybe not too soon?"

He bent and hooked the backs of her thighs and lifted her.

She wrapped her legs around his waist and pressed her center against the ridge beneath the fly of his jeans. "One for the road?"

He nuzzled her neck. "As long as you can reach into the nightstand."

Beth leaned over, pulled open the drawer and fished out another special packet.

"Good girl." Dawg carried her into the dining room and sat her on the edge of the table where they'd had dinner. "We'll call it dessert." He unzipped his fly. When his cock sprang free, he leaned back and let her apply the condom to his engorged staff. Her hands on him made him even harder and more determined to have her again.

Once she'd sheathed him, Beth guided him to her entrance and scooted to the edge of the table, giving him more access.

He slid into her warmth. She felt so very good wrapped tightly around him, making him swell inside her.

Then he moved. Slowly at first, then building up speed as he pumped in and out of her.

With her dress hitched up around her waist, she leaned back on her hands, her head tipped back, her eyes closed.

He reached between them and fondled her clit, stroking it with his fingers, flicking the little nubbin of flesh until her breathing grew ragged and her channel tightened around his cock.

ELLE JAMES

When she cried out her release, he slammed into her once more and held onto her hips as he rode his orgasm to the end.

He kissed her again, pulled free and stripped the condom off, dropping it into the trash.

Once he'd washed his hands, he retrieved Beth's panties from the other room and found her shoes beside the couch.

She still sat on the edge of the table. "I don't think my legs will hold me," she said with a grin.

"Then allow me." He slid her panties over her feet and ankles and up her long legs as far as he could while she remained seated. Then he slipped her shoes onto her feet and pulled her off the table, standing her in front of him. When she swayed, he slipped his arms around her and held her close. "I need to get you to your place so you can get some sleep."

"I can sleep on the flight to wherever the hell I'm going," she said.

"And you still don't know where you're headed?"

Beth shook her head. "I won't know until the briefing tomorrow. And then, maybe, only the continent." She snorted. "It's all hush-hush."

Once she was steady on her feet, he reached beneath her dress, pulled her panties in place then stepped back and offered his hand.

She took it and let him lead her toward the door.

Chewy was up and trotting beside them, eager to go wherever they went.

"Sorry, buddy," Dawg said. "You have to stay. I'll be right back."

When Dawg looked up, he caught Beth smiling at him, the light dancing in her eyes.

"What's so funny?" he asked.

"Nothing. I just think it's cute that you talk to your dog."

He held up his other hand. "Doesn't everyone who has a dog?"

Beth frowned. "I can't imagine my ex talking to a dog. He barely talks to his patients. He only spares enough conversation to diagnose."

"Not much of a bedside manner?"

She shook her head. "Not much of one. But he's amazing at diagnosing and treating people."

He led her out to his truck and helped her up into it. Once he climbed in beside her, he glanced across the console and into her eyes. "I don't want to take you home."

"I could call for a cab or Uber," she suggested. "There's no need for you to go out this late."

He shook his head, a smile teasing the corners of his lips. "No, it's not that, it's not wanting to end this evening. I know we won't see each other for a long time." He started the vehicle and pulled out onto the street in front of his house. "I'm just getting to know you. I'd like a little more time."

"But we go when we have to," she whispered.

The rest of the drive was made in silence.

When Dawg pulled up to her apartment building, he shifted into park and started to get out.

Beth laid a hand on his arm. "Stay here. I can see myself to my own door."

When he opened his mouth to argue, she shook her head. "Seriously. It's hard enough parting like this."

He reached out and cupped her cheek. "If only we weren't deploying in the next couple of days..."

She covered his hand with hers and leaned her cheek into his palm. "It's not goodbye. I refuse to let it be."

He brushed his thumb across her lips. "I hope you'll consider going out on another date with me when we're both back stateside."

She nodded. "I'd like that." Beth leaned across the console and kissed him long and hard.

He captured the back of her head and deepened the kiss.

When he let go, she slipped out of the truck and ran across the parking lot to her door. Moments later, she was inside with the door closed between them.

For the next few minutes, Dawg sat in his truck staring at Beth's apartment door, wondering when he'd gone from liking the pretty nurse to falling in love with her.

Now that they were being separated by their duties, he wondered if they'd ever get back together. Or had what they'd experienced that night only been a dream, never to happen again?

CHAPTER 5

BETH ARRIVED in Nigeria thirty-six hours after she'd left Dawg sitting in his truck outside her apartment. She'd cried all the way into her house and throughout the process of completing her packing. She'd had exactly three hours sleep before she'd gotten up, loaded her car and driven to where her commander had arranged for her to view the country and mission assignment briefing.

They hadn't told her much about the mission or who she'd be working with. Apparently, the mission had begun months before, but they'd had to send one of the nurses back who'd contracted an infection and needed time for it to heal Stateside. She would take that nurse's place for the duration of the mission.

The team she'd be working with had a doctor, several medics and a helicopter crew that would fly their patients in and, sometimes, fly the team out to wherever they were needed. She didn't know who she'd be working with and wouldn't until she landed at the forward operating base.

The area they were headed was hot with terrorists. The medical team would be there in support of a Special Forces detachment that was in the area to help the indigenous forces learn how to protect their population.

She was given several inoculations, extra uniforms and a nine-millimeter pistol she was to carry at all times. Thankfully, she'd been to the firing range recently to familiarize with the weapon. The medical staff at the Fort Hood Army Hospital didn't have much need for weapons in their hospital duties. Qualifying once a year or once every other year didn't make her an expert, but at least she knew how to load, fire and set the handgun on safe when she wasn't using it. And she could break it down, clean it and reassemble the weapon, when needed.

A medic, Sergeant Graves, and his Private First Class driver had met her at the airport when she'd landed in Kanos. She'd been told to wear civilian clothing for the flight. Her medic and his driver also wore civilian clothing. The medic handed her a light blue hijab and told her she'd need to wear it whenever she was around the Nigerians. Then he led her to a rental car. They drove twenty miles beyond the city to a dry stretch of desert and stopped. Minutes later, a Black Hawk helicopter landed.

Beth and her escorts climbed into the helicopter and flew the rest of the way to the location where she'd be working.

Exhausted by the long flights and secrecy, Beth was ready to find her quarters, be it a tent or a hut, and sleep. She doubted that would happen. With the unit being one nurse down, she expected to have to hit the ground running if they had a heavy patient load.

The helicopter landed near a small village of stick and mud huts and a small group of Army tents hidden beneath desert camouflage netting. The netting helped hide the tents from aircraft and drones and provided a small amount of shade for the people beneath.

The medic led her through the maze to a single hospital tent. "The doc will want to brief you on the mission before you start," the medic said. "If you need anything, let me know what it is, and I'll see if we have it in supply." He gave her a brief smile. "Welcome to Camp Iguana." He started to leave.

"Sergeant Graves," she stopped him with her voice.

He turned. "Yes, ma'am?"

"The doctor? Where do I find him?"

The sergeant tipped his head toward her, looking over her shoulder. "Behind you, ma'am."

Beth spun to face the doctor in charge of the medical staff, and her heart sank to her knees.

"Jonathan," she said, her head spinning. Her ex-fiancé was the last person she'd expected to see that day and the last one she wanted to see. "I mean, Colonel Parker, sir." She stood at attention in front of the man she was supposed to have married six months before, her stomach queasy, her hands shaking.

He gave her half a smile. "Beth. I'm glad you made it without incident."

She frowned. "You act as if you were expecting me. Did you know I would be the one coming?"

He held out his hands. "I asked for you, specifically."

Beth stepped backward, out of his reach, her frown deepening. "Why would you do that?"

His hands dropped to his sides. "I know you. You're one of the best nurses I've ever worked with. Anyone else, I'd be taking a chance with. I know how steady and unflappable you are. This place can be dangerous. I needed someone who could handle it without coming apart."

Her lips pressed into a thin line. "Is that why they didn't tell me anything about who I'd be working with?"

"Partly. I didn't think you'd come if you knew I was the one who'd be in charge."

"You're damn right I wouldn't have come," she said.

"I needed a good nurse."

But he didn't need her. Her reasons for ending their engagement still stood. Jonathan's focus, as always, was solely on his work. Which wasn't a bad thing for the people he helped. But Beth wanted more than parttime affection from the man she would marry. She wanted a man who cared about how she felt and wanted her to care about him. He wasn't that person. The man she thought she'd fallen in love with wasn't the man for her. He was an excellent doctor who would remain married to his field.

"*Because it was me* wasn't the only reason I didn't want them to tell you," he continued. "I also couldn't have them tell you who you'd be working with partly because this is a secret assignment. The less anyone knows about it, the better. We're not supposed to be here. We're calling this a humanitarian mission. We help a few of the locals, but we're here for the Special Forces guys. They're here to train the Nigerian military to protect their own people."

"Well," Beth said. "I'm here now. How many beds do you have in this hospital?"

"Four," he answered. "But we have enough

supplies to bring it up to six. Our task isn't to keep our soldiers here, but to stabilize them and move them on to the next level of care."

Beth nodded. That was how they'd worked in Afghanistan. If injuries were severe, the medical staff were to stabilize the patient and move them on to places like Landstuhl, Germany, where the surgical staff had more resources to handle difficult cases. Ultimately, the patient was sent back to the States for the specialists and long-term recovery.

"Anyone in your beds now?" she asked.

Jonathan shook his head. "No. But we have a makeshift hospital for the locals in the village. "I'm headed there now if you want to join me."

Feeling a bit in a fog from lack of sleep, Beth would have preferred to find her quarters and grab a couple hours of sleep. It was still daylight, and it was hot. The lack of air conditioning would keep her from sleeping for a couple days until her body adjusted. She might as well do the rounds with the doctor, ignoring the fact he was her ex-fiancé. Beth was a professional. She could work with the man without dwelling on what should have or could have been between them.

She drew in a deep breath and let it out. "Lead the way." Beth followed Jonathan out of the Army encampment and into the little village nearby.

A long, low building on the edge of the village

had a line of Nigerians standing outside it. Men, women and children waited for medical care.

"This building was a school for the children," Jonathan said. "When Boko Haram threatened to burn it to the ground, they moved their school out of the building and into the open under the trees, making this a hospital. We've trained some of the locals to help with the people who come seeking medical help. Between the locals, our medics and myself, we see as many patients as possible in a couple of hours each day. The Red Cross has provided limited medical supplies, antibiotics and much-needed vaccinations.

"Most of these people have no other medical services available to them. Some need stitches, some need teeth pulled. Others need antibiotics. We have to be careful distributing the antibiotics as there just isn't enough to treat everyone."

"There never seems to be enough in places like this. Especially, when they're under attack and the supplies are stolen by the terrorists," Beth noted.

Jonathan nodded. "We were expecting another shipment of medical supplies from the Red Cross a couple of days ago. We got word the truck the supplies were on was captured, the drivers killed and the supplies taken by Boko Haram terrorists."

Beth shook her head. "What's keeping them from attacking this outpost?"

"The Special Forces who are collocated with us."

As they neared the makeshift hospital, the people waiting to see the doctor reached out to touch him as if he were some kind of saint there to heal them. To them, he might as well be a saint or god. When they'd run out of all the natural remedies they could come up with on their own, they put their faith in one man whose reputation was spreading to other villages.

Beth could understand their desire to touch him. For people who were sick or in pain, he represented hope.

They had to duck to enter the hut. Inside was dark except where windows were open to let in fresh air.

A dark man wearing a white T-shirt stood just inside the door. He dipped his head toward the doctor.

"Beth, this is Ekong, one of the locals who can speak a little English. He works as my interpreter."

Beth nodded. "Nice to meet you."

The man's head dipped. "You are the new nurse?"

Beth smiled. "I am."

"You help the good doctor?" he asked.

"I will," Beth answered.

"Good. Good."

Jonathan stepped past him. "We have ten beds on the other side of the curtain," he said. "All ten beds are occupied. Hopefully, two of the patients will be well enough to go home today. I'll do my rounds first, then we'll see the patients waiting at the door."

They passed through the front room where two medics waited beside portable Army desks. They stood at parade rest until Jonathan stepped up to them and they came to attention.

"PFC Miller and Corporal Ramsey, this is Lieutenant Drennan, our new nurse."

"Ma'am," the two medics said as one.

"We're glad you're here, ma'am" Corporal Ramsey said. "We've been without a nurse for a couple days."

"Nice to meet you," she said. "I look forward to working with you."

Jonathan led the way past the medics and pushed aside the curtain to reveal two rows of beds filled with patients.

One by one, they stopped at the beds that consisted of Army cots.

Beth helped to reapply bandages and clean infection sites.

At six feet tall, Jonathan had to stoop to use his stethoscope to listen to heartbeats or check a dressing. The two men at the far end of the building sat on the edges of their cots.

Jonathan checked them over and spoke quietly to the interpreter, asking questions and listening to their responses. He was quick and didn't spend more time than was necessary. When he was done, the two men gathered their belongings.

Corporal Ramsey hurried into the ward to help one of the men limp to the exit. The other man walked out on his own where his family was waiting to help him get home.

Beth watched as the two men departed. "What do you do if they don't have family waiting to help them home?"

"Some of the locals have vehicles. They help those that they can. Other patients don't have homes to go to. They've set up a kind of refugee camp on the other side of the village. Boko Haram destroyed their villages, leaving them homeless."

"How do they survive?" Beth asked, her heart going out to the men, women and children displaced by the actions of others in a war they hadn't asked for.

"Donations sent by other countries," the interpreter said. "When they are not captured by thieves."

After rounds of the beds was complete, they saw the patients waiting outside. The medics had conducted a quick triage of those present. The most critical were directed to Jonathan.

Beth assisted when needed and dealt with those she could handle on her own.

By the time they finished, it was getting dark. Beth's belly rumbled.

"We should eat. I'm sorry to say our meals consist mostly of MREs."

"Considering the refugees get less than that, I won't complain," Beth said.

Jonathan nodded. "It's fuel for our bodies. Even if it's tasteless."

Beth sighed. "I'll get used to it again."

They returned to the Army camp, grabbed a packet of MREs and sat at a table beneath the camouflage netting to eat, washing down the food with bottled water. The sun was setting and shadows lengthening.

Though exhausted, Beth stayed awake long enough to choke down some of the food, while sitting across from the man she'd almost married.

"What went wrong with us?" Jonathan asked, echoing Beth's thoughts.

She stared across the table at him. "I'm really tired from my trip here. Now might not be a good time to ask that question." The fact that he had to ask said it all. He was clueless about how to make her happy. All she'd wanted was a little of his attention, a level of commitment equal to hers. But he truly didn't see anything wrong with what he'd done by volunteering to go on a mission that would make them move their wedding date yet again... two weeks before they'd been about say I do.

For weeks after she'd called off the wedding,

Beth had wondered if she'd made the right choice. She'd wondered if she was being selfish by putting herself and their marriage before the health and welfare of others. The first time he'd forced her to change their wedding date, she'd been okay. The second time, only two weeks before the ceremony...on a voluntary basis...no.

"You're right. The trip here is exhausting. You need to get some rest." He reached across the table and took her hand. "I'm glad you're here."

And in an instant, she was back to second-guessing her decision to call off the wedding. When he did pay attention to her, it was good.

But now, there was someone else in the picture. A man she'd slept with. One who made her burn with desire, unlike Jonathan. Their lovemaking had been good, but not anything as earth-shaking as what she'd experienced with Dawg.

On the other hand, if she married Jonathan, she wouldn't have the Army shaking a finger at her about an officer fraternizing with the enlisted ranks.

The powers that be frowned on officers dating enlisted men. That hadn't stopped her from going out with Dawg or Nora from falling in love with Rucker. As long as they weren't in the same chain of command, the Army couldn't do anything.

Still, it would be easier to be in a relationship

with an officer. She wouldn't have to worry about rank.

Dawg was a Delta Force operative. He'd be gone as much, if not more, than Jonathan. If she dated and then married him, he'd be gone all the time.

That had never been the issue with her and Jonathan. Being gone was something you learned to accept as part of wearing the uniform. It was the fact that Jonathan hadn't had to go both times he'd asked her to postpone the wedding. Both times, he'd volunteered to go. Other doctors could have taken his place.

But he'd chosen his work over marrying her. Perhaps, subconsciously, he hadn't wanted to marry her.

Beth stared across the table at the man. He was handsome, in an intellectual way. Dawg was handsome in a rugged, physical way.

Being with Jonathan made her think about them as a couple. Had he learned anything from her calling off the wedding? Did he want her back? If he was willing to commit this time, would she take him back?

And what about the incredible sex she'd had with Dawg before she'd left Texas?

Her head ached with all the thoughts swimming around.

"I think I'll find my quarters and call it a night."

Corporal Ramsey suddenly appeared beside

Jonathan. "Colonel Parker, sir, one of the Nigerian Special Forces men is asking for you."

Jonathan frowned. "Is he injured?"

"No, sir," Ramsey said. "He's brought his wife."

"Is she injured?"

"No, sir." Ramsey shook his head. "Well, not yet. You see, sir, she's pregnant and in labor."

"They have midwives to help them through childbirth. Why did he bring her here?"

"I think the baby's breech," the medic said. "Ekong said she's in terrible pain and has been that way for over twenty-four hours. What do you want me to do?"

"Bring her to our hospital. I'll check her." Jonathan pushed to his feet and looked across the table to Beth. "You don't have to assist if you're too tired."

Beth shook her head. "I'd like to help if I can."

Jonathan didn't respond but walked out of the mess area and headed for the hospital tent.

A couple of Nigerian men carried the pregnant woman in a fireman's carry, sitting between their arms.

The woman's eyes were squeezed shut and her body tensed through a contraction. She cried out as they sat her on the edge of one of the hospital beds.

The medic had the men clear out of the room, except for the woman's husband. He gave the man a choice of staying or leaving. The man chose to leave, holding his hands up and shaking his head as he backed away from his wife.

Beth figured the man thought of birthing as woman's work. It was just as well he left. If the baby was breech, they'd have to turn the baby or perform a cesarian-section and cut the baby out of the woman's belly. Either way would be painful for her. But at that point, she was already in pain and willing to do just about anything to make it stop.

For the next couple of hours, Jonathan worked with the woman. Beth monitored the baby's heartbeat, watching for signs the baby was in distress.

Given the conditions, a Cesarian-section was risky, especially for recovery.

Jonathan wouldn't do it unless it was a last resort. "We need to try turning the baby first," he said. "Beth, are you familiar with an ECV— External Cephalic Version?"

She nodded. "Yes. I know what it is and have witnessed it twice. It's about fifty percent successful."

"I'll take those odds to deliver this baby naturally. I'm willing to bet a C-section would put the mother at too much risk of infection."

If they could get the baby turned around, nature would take its course and the baby would deliver head-first.

Jonathan spoke to the interpreter, telling him what the woman could expect. After Ekong passed on the information, Jonathan laid his hands on the woman's belly and applied firm pressure, kneading the baby beneath, guiding it to a head-down position.

The woman's body tensed as she experienced another contraction.

Beth stood near the woman's head, stared into her eyes until she returned the gaze. Then Beth showed her how to breathe to ease the pain, encouraging her to do as Beth was doing.

They didn't have the tools or medications to give the woman an epidural for pain, so she had to manage the pain herself.

Jonathan and Beth worked into the night, trying to turn the baby. When it finally shifted in her belly into a head-down position, Beth wanted to cheer out loud.

By then, the mother was so tired, she didn't have the strength to push.

Beth held the mother's hand as the next contraction wracked her body. She helped the exhausted women to halfway sit up for a better position to push the baby out.

After several more contractions, the baby's head presented.

With each contraction, Beth pushed the mother up to a sitting position and encouraged her to bear down.

Tears streamed from the woman's eyes, but

Beth wouldn't let her give up. That baby had to come out soon. Already the baby's heart was showing signs of distress.

"Come on, Mama, you can do it," Beth said.

On the next contraction, the baby's head slid out.

Jonathan helped his shoulders through and the rest of his little body slid right out into Jonathan's hands. He cut the umbilical cord and handed the baby over to Corporal Ramsey.

The medic wiped down the baby with a clean cloth and laid it on the mother's chest.

Beth massaged the woman's belly while Jonathan delivered the placenta and checked it over for completeness. After the mother had a chance to be with her baby, Beth took the baby from her arms and laid him in a jerry-rigged bassinet made of a cardboard box with a clean sheet draped around the inside.

By the time it was all said and done, the woman had her baby, the baby was healthy and alive, and so was the mother.

When Beth stepped out of the hospital tent, the gray light of morning was pushing away the darkness of night.

Beyond tired, Beth knew she wouldn't sleep until she burned off some of the adrenaline that she'd run on during the delivery of the baby.

She asked Corporal Ramsey where her duffel

bag had been taken. He gave her directions to find her way through the maze of tents. A few minutes later, she'd found her tent and her duffel bag inside. She quickly changed from her dirty travel clothing to a pair of shorts and her running shoes, pulled her hair back into a ponytail and secured it with an elastic band.

Feeling a little better, she jogged around the perimeter of the Army encampment. It wasn't a large enough area to burn off the adrenaline she still had racing through her system, so she struck out on a road leading away from the camp and away from the village. She only intended to go a little way, turn around and come back.

She wasn't far from the camp when she noticed someone running behind her.

Beth knew better than to go running by herself and especially in a foreign country. But she'd been so tired, her ability to think logically had been severely impaired.

Now that she was being followed, her focus became crystal clear. She had to get back to camp.

Unfortunately, whoever was following her was between her and camp.

Beth ran faster, knowing it was taking her even farther away from safety.

What else could she do? She'd left her gun on her cot.

CHAPTER 6

"I'M HITTING THE SACK," Rucker said. "I suggest you all find a place to sleep and get some rest. The team we're replacing has been working this area hard. They haven't had much time to sit back and relax."

"Wasn't very friendly the last time we came to this country," Bull commented.

"I'm sure we didn't make any friends by taking out the Boko Haram leader."

"Too bad we didn't get them all," Blade said. "I hear the one they have now is even worse than Kalani."

"Great. Gives us something to shoot at," Tank dropped his go-bag outside one of the designated tents. "I call this one."

Dawg ducked into another of the unoccupied tents, dropped his bag and dug out a pair of shorts and his running shoes. He was changed in less than a minute, strapped on his shoulder holster, tucked his nine-millimeter pistol into the holster and was back outside into the early morning light before the others could choose their tents and get settled in.

"I need to burn off some energy," Dawg said. "I'm going for a run."

"Stay close to camp," Rucker advised. "We haven't gotten the local briefing yet. We don't know who's friend and who's foe until then."

Dawg nodded. "I won't go far. And I've got my weapon."

"Want me to go with you?" Mac asked.

"No. I need the quiet," Dawg was tired, but he wanted to think about Beth and the night they'd spent together before she'd left. Hell, he'd done nothing but think about her since he'd left her at her apartment.

"I'd prefer you took a buddy," Rucker said.

"I won't go far," Dawg said. "Just around the encampment. Within shouting distance."

"Okay then, go," Rucker waved a hand. "I'm too tired to argue. Don't get yourself killed. I don't want to do the paperwork."

Dawg grinned and set off jogging. He made four passes around the camp before he struck out along a road leading away from the camp.

Moving helped his body get over being crammed in the back of a C-130 Hercules, hanging from the web seats the entire trip from Texas to Rota, Spain. Afterward, they'd flown from Rota across the continent to Nigeria. He was tired and aching from the rides. Running helped to loosen stiff muscles and clear his head.

Ahead, he noticed a man running. He wasn't wearing a uniform, and he was as dark as night. When the man dodged around a big pothole in the dirt road, Dawg noticed another figure ahead of him running, and it appeared to be a female who was looking over her shoulder. Was she running away from the man behind her?

Dawg picked up speed, slowly catching up to the man in front of him, which wasn't easy. The guy had speed going for him. The woman in front of him was slowing. She couldn't stay ahead of him.

But she sure as hell was trying.

Adrenaline spiked and fueled Dawg's steps.

By the time the man was within five feet of the woman, Dawg caught him and raced past him.

He caught up with the woman, grabbed her arm, spun her around and turned at the same time to face her pursuer.

When he did, the man skidded to a halt, switched directions and darted into the under-brush alongside the road.

Dawg held his gun in his hand and faced the direction the man had disappeared.

Out of the corner of his eye, he watched the

woman he'd stopped, as she bent over, dragging deep gulps of breath into her lungs. "Hey, are you okay?"

When her breathing slowed enough, she straightened, nodding. "Thanks," she said and turned to face him.

Dawg swore. "Beth?"

"Dawg?" Beth laughed. "What are you doing here?"

He chuckled. "I was going to ask you the same thing."

She pulled the ponytail out of her hair and shook it loose. "What were the odds that we'd deploy to the exact same place?"

Dawg pulled her into his arms. "Well, I for one am glad to see you."

She hugged him back, her breathing still labored but more in control. "Not as glad as I am to see you." Beth leaned back and frowned toward the brush. "I didn't know how I was going to get back to camp with that guy chasing after me."

Dawg dropped his arms from around her and took one of her hands, still holding his gun in the other. "Let's get you back before he decides to bring some of his friends back with him."

"I was stupid to go out on my own," she admitted. "I have to remember I'm not back in Texas, and some of these people would just as soon slit your throat as anything." Beth sighed. "I need sleep."

"Slit your throat or worse," Dawg's brow furrowed. "He could've sold you into the sex trade. It's big business in this country."

"Yeah, well I won't go out on my own again. That was a bit terrifying." She squeezed his hand. "Thank you again. You saved my life."

"Which makes me responsible for you now." He shook his head. "That will be a challenge when I'm out fighting bad guys, and you're back here."

"I promise to stay closer to camp from now on," she said. "And you don't have to be responsible for me."

"It's an old Chinese proverb. You can't change tradition." As they neared the camp, he let go of her hand. "I can start by not getting you in trouble for fraternizing while in theater." He winked. "I'll have to wait to kiss you again until we get back to the States. You promised me a date."

She smiled. "I did. Or did you promise me a date?"

"I think it was mutual. And the sooner we tie up this mission, the better."

They ducked beneath the camouflage netting.

"Where are you headed now?"

"The mess area for some yummy MREs?" she said. "Care to join me?"

"I could use some hardening of the arteries."

At that moment, they passed the hospital tent.

A man emerged from the tent and frowned, his

gaze going from Dawg to Beth. "Beth? Are you okay?"

Beth's face turned pink. "I'm fine."

Again, the man's gaze went from Beth to Dawg and back to Beth. "Do you two know each other?"

"Yes," Dawg said.

"No," Beth said at the same time. "I mean, we know each other, but we don't *know* each other."

The man's brow wrinkled.

Beth laughed, the sound strained. "He's from Fort Hood. We've run into each other before." She turned to Dawg. "Sergeant Doug Masters, this is Doctor...er...Colonel Jonathan Parker, the camp surgeon." She smiled brightly. "There. Now, you two know each other."

What was wrong with Beth? Her mouth was tight and she wrung her hands more than once while standing there. And it had something to do with the doctor. If Dawg wasn't mistaken, she wasn't happy about the two men meeting. Dawg grinned. "We were just about to get something for breakfast. Would you care to join us?"

Colonel Parker's brow wrinkled for a moment.

Beth chewed on her bottom lip; something Dawg had noticed she did when she was nervous.

"Sure," Colonel Parker said. "I could do with a bite to eat, and I wouldn't mind the company."

Out of the corner of his eye, Dawg saw Beth roll her eyes.

Who was this man, other than the camp surgeon? And why was she so tense about them meeting? Was she afraid he'd suspect that they were fraternizing? The man was obviously her superior officer. But their relationship appeared to be more than that.

All the more reason to have breakfast with the man and find out what had Beth tied in a knot.

They didn't have far to go to arrive at tables that had been set up for the dining area. They selected packets of MREs and chose seats.

Beth sat beside Colonel Parker. Dawg sat across from the two, studying their faces as he tore open the packet of Spaghetti with Beef and Sauce. He could almost pretend it was the Chicken Parmesan he'd made for his date with the nurse sitting across the table from him.

"You're not with the medical or supply staff, are you?" Colonel Parker asked.

"No, sir," Dawg replied. "We came in early this morning as replacements for the Delta Force Team who've been here for the past six months."

The other man nodded. "I see. When will the current team ship out?"

"I'm not sure," Dawg said. "Probably soon. What about you? How long have you been here, sir?"

"A little over six months."

Dawg cocked an eyebrow. "Will they be sending a replacement for you soon?"

"I assume so," he said.

"You don't sound like you're ready to go," Dawg said

"I feel like I have more to do here." Colonel Parker glanced toward Beth.

Something clicked in Dawg. "Did you volunteer for this mission, or were you *voluntold* to come?"

Beside the doctor Beth stiffened and her eyes narrowed, drilling into Dawg.

"They needed a flight surgeon." Colonel Parker shrugged. "I volunteered."

Dawg grinned. Now, it all made sense. "Didn't your family have heartburn with your decision?"

"I don't have any family," Dr Parker struggled to open one of the food packets within the big packet.

Beth's mouth firmed into a thin line.

The doctor shot a glance toward her. "I mean, I had a fiancée, but she wasn't very happy about me going."

"*Had* a fiancée?" Dawg raised both eyebrows. "What happened?"

Colonel Parker shot another glance toward Beth. "I guess I didn't fight hard enough. I lost her."

"That's too bad," Dawg murmured while Beth glared at him. "How could a woman call off an engagement to a man like you? That doesn't give men like me any hope at all."

"You're gone a lot, too," the doctor noted. "How does your family handle it?"

"I don't have a family, but someday I hope to." Dawg caught Beth's stare and gave her a wink while Colonel Parker was looking down at his meal packets.

The color in her cheeks darkened.

"Beth, aren't you going to eat?" the doctor asked her.

"I'm too tired," she said. "I think I'll leave you two to this fascinating conversation and grab me some shuteye before I fall on my face."

When she stood, Dawg stood.

Colonel Parker frowned and slowly rose to his feet. "I'll see you this afternoon as I do my rounds and village sick call...?"

She nodded. "I'll be there. I just need a good six hours sleep before then." She smiled at Colonel Parker. "And congratulations on delivering that breech baby. You were amazing."

The doctor's frown deepened. "I did what any doctor would have done."

"And in the process, you saved two lives." Beth touched his shoulder. "You did good, sir."

He nodded. "Thank you."

Beth left the two men facing off across the table from each other and walked away.

Dawg's gaze shifted to Beth as she walked away. He noticed Colonel Parker's gaze also following the pretty nurse.

"She's good at what she does," the doctor said.

"We're lucky to have her here."

"I take it you two have worked together before," Dawg stated.

Colonel Parker nodded. "We worked at the hospital on Fort Hood. That's where we met two years ago. She's an excellent surgical nurse, always anticipating the surgeon's needs before he asks."

"Good skills to have when the doctor needs to focus his attention on saving lives," Dawg said.

"That's right," Parker said. "That's why I requested her for this mission."

"You requested her specifically?" Dawg's attention was caught. "And she came running because of her experience working with you?"

Colonel Parker shook his head. "Not exactly. We had a falling out awhile back. I told her commander not to tell her who requested her. I didn't think she'd come."

Already knowing what the fallout was, Dawg asked anyway to get Parker's take on what had occurred. "What happened between the two of you that would make her say no to joining you on a mission?"

Colonel Parker stared off into the distance. "I'm not exactly sure. One minute we were fine. The next she cut me off completely. I was hoping that having her out here would not only help the mission succeed, but also give me time to figure out what I did that made her mad, so I can fix it." He turned his gaze to Dawg. "What about you? Do you have a wife and kids back home?"

"No. But I met a woman I think is pretty amazing."

"That's great. Is it serious?" Colonel Parker met Dawg's gaze.

"I don't know yet. She was pretty hurt in a past relationship. I don't know if she's over the other guy. I think if he's the right guy for her, she needs to give him a second chance. But if he's not, I hope she'll give me a chance."

Parker's lips quirked upward. "She must be special for you to want her to be happy either way she goes."

"She is," Dawg said.

"That's how I feel about Beth. She's special. I didn't know how special until she wasn't there anymore." He turned his head away again and stared out at the landscape visible beneath the edge of the camouflage canopy. "She's the best nurse."

"Is that all she is to you, a good nurse?"

Colonel Parker turned to face him. "For this mission, we can't be anything more than that. I'm her commander." He collected his empty packets and the ones he hadn't opened. A trash can stood at the end of the outdoor dining area. Beside it was a box. "Please let your teammates know that we donate the unused, unopened MRE packets to the refugee camp. They might be the only meal they get today."

After the doctor left the dining area, Dawg sat for a few minutes longer, staring out at the landscape, trying to see what Parker had seen. The man was empathetic to the plights of others. If he was a competent doctor, he had a lot more to offer Beth than an enlisted Delta.

Dawg gathered his trash and tossed it into the garbage container. The rest of his meal ended up in the donation box to go to the refugee camp. The medical staff was doing the right things to help the locals in exchange for a place to base their operations. Free healthcare, food and the protection of Delta Force.

From the briefings they'd receive in route, the Boko Haram leader Dawg and his team had disposed of had been replaced by his second in command, the man who'd escaped in the SUV that night. Rucker had sworn when he'd heard that bit of intelligence. "We should've taken him out that night."

Dawg had reminded Rucker that if it hadn't been the second in command, it would've been someone else. Unless they wiped out all of the members of Boko Haram, the group would remain a problem.

Rucker knew that. The entire team knew it. Cutting off the head of the snake only slowed them down. They were back to the same terrorist activities as before, burning down villages, kidnapping school kids and aid workers and holding them hostage for hefty ransoms.

Thus, the return of the Deltas to take Dawg's team's place when they'd left after killing Kalani.

They were in one of the most dangerous areas of Africa, where Boko Haram had pretty much taken over. The Nigerian government had given up on the northeast corner of the country.

Dawg strode through camp and found the tent he would share with Blade, Tank and Dash. The three men had gone right to sleep, knowing they might be called to fight at any moment. A Delta had to know how to work the mission, but he also had to know when to sleep and recharge his internal batteries.

Dawg pulled off his uniform jacket and stretched out on the only empty cot left. He laced his hands behind his head and closed his eyes to the midday light making its way beneath the rolled up flaps of the tent. If not for the camouflage netting above the tents, the heat of the day would've baked the roof of the tent, and the Deltas beneath it. As it was, the heat was oppressive, even in the shade cast by the netting.

Dawg forced his mind to shut down. He needed to conserve energy and recharge his body after the long flight from the States to Rota,

Spain, and then to Nigeria. The Delta team they were to replace hadn't been there to welcome them. They were out on maneuvers, looking for the Boko Haram compound that moved often enough, even the satellites had a hard time finding them.

Despite the sweat dripping off his forehead, he drifted into a troubled sleep, where terrorists burned the village around Dawg, Beth and her ex-fiancé. Dawg yelled at the doctor to get Beth out of the fire, but the doctor was too busy trying to save a dying local to worry about his nurse.

Dawg dove through the fire, swept Beth up in his arms and walked back through the flames. Neither he nor Beth caught fire, but their skin was hot and their passion hotter.

When he woke, the sun was already on its way down to the western horizon, the shadows lengthening.

Blade was pulling on his uniform jacket. Tank had left the tent, and Dash was just rolling out of his cot.

"I could stand some coffee and some chow," Dash said with a yawn. "I'm groggy as hell after that nap."

"Coffee first," Blade agreed. "You'd think Tank would've at least come back and told us where we could find sustenance."

"I can show you to the dining area and the box

of MREs you'll be interested in," Dawg said with a sarcastic tilt to his lips.

"Oh, good. MREs. My favorite." Blade snorted. "If I ever go to work for Hank Patterson and the Brotherhood Protectors, it'll be on the condition that I never have to eat another packet of Meals Ready to Eat."

"Amen," Dash yawned. "Until we leave this side of Hell, I take it that's all we have available?" His gaze found Dawg.

Dawg nodded. "There's no mess hall, and I doubt we want to eat local cuisine or drink the water. They do have cases of water near the outdoor dining area. You'll want to fill your canteens with that, versus the well water here."

"On it," Blade said. "Point me in the right direction." He stepped out of the tent.

"Take a right and keep walking." Dawg said. "You can't miss the tables they set up and the crate of MREs waiting for your enjoyment."

Blade left the tent. Dash pulled on his uniform shirt and headed out. He paused just outside the tent and looked back. "You coming?"

"I'll catch up in a minute. I want to find the latrine."

Dash nodded and left Dawg to his own devices.

Dawg did want to locate the latrine but, more importantly, he wanted to find Beth.

Grabbing his toiletry kit, he made his way to

what appeared to be the shower facility, outside which was a lister bag filled with water, a clean bowl and a mirror. He took a few minutes to brush his teeth, comb his hair and use the latrine. When he was done, he returned his toiletry kit to his quarters and made his way to the hospital tent.

A medic sat at a desk just inside the tent flap. "May I help you, sir?"

"I was looking for Lieutenant Drennan."

The medic shook his head. "The nurse went with the doctor to the village hospital to make their rounds. They should be back shortly. Are you feeling sick? Or do you have an injury that needs to be tended?" His hands hovered over a laptop, waiting for Dawg's response.

"Neither. I just had a question for her." Dawg dipped his head. "Thanks." He left the hospital tent and walked down to the dining area where he found his team gathered around the table. "About time you showed up," Rucker said.

"Have you heard anything from the other Delta team?" Dawg asked.

Rucker frowned. "Not yet. They've been out a long time."

Just then, the thumping sound of rotor blades filled the sky as a Black Hawk helicopter swooped in and slowly descended for a landing in the clearing nearby.

Rucker stood, gathered his food packets and

dumped the empties in the garbage, the full in the donation box. He wiped his hands together, his gaze on the helicopter as the wheels touched the ground. "I'll go find out what's going on."

Dawg stepped up beside the team leader. "We're coming with you."

Mac, Blade, Tank, Bull, Dash and Lance scrambled to clear their trash and hurried to catch up.

As soon as the craft settled, a soldier leaped to the ground and ran toward the camp. He skidded to a stop in front of Rucker. "Are you the new Delta replacements?"

Rucker nodded.

"Get your weapons and load up on ammo," the man said. "Team Charlie could use some help."

CHAPTER 7

BETH HAD MANAGED to sleep for four hours straight before the heat of the afternoon sun woke her and sent her in search of a shower and a drink of water. A slight headache had reminded her she needed to stay hydrated. The low humidity would dry her sweat so fast she wouldn't know she was dehydrated until it was too late.

With a water bottle in hand, she'd found Jonathan. Together, they'd checked the new mother and released her from the camp hospital to go home. Other than being sore, she was feeling fine. The baby was nursing with a healthy appetite. They'd done all they could do for the pair. She'd return to her home that day and leave the camp hospital empty. The medic would clean and sterilize the bed, sheets and equipment for the next patient.

"Ready to make the rounds at the village hospital?" Jonathan asked

Beth nodded and followed him out of the camp and into the village. As it had been the day before, a line had formed outside the mud and stick building.

Inside, they saw to the eight patients in the beds.

Corporal Ramsey reported on the progress of each.

Jonathan spoke to each man via the interpreter. Three more of the patients were well enough to go home.

Sick call was as busy as it had been the day before.

"Are there always so many?" Beth asked between the tenth and eleventh patient.

"No," Jonathan squirted anti-bacterial gel into his hands and rubbed them together. "Sometimes, there are more. This is a light day."

After they saw the last patient for the day, Jonathan left the medics to help the locals clean up. He cupped Beth's elbow and walked with her back to the Army camp. As they walked, he turned to her. "What happened to us, Beth?" he asked. "Why did you break our engagement?"

Beth shook her head. "If you have to ask, you don't know me well enough to marry me." Six months had given her time to get over her anger and to try to understand what had really gone wrong between them. "And I admit, I didn't know you well enough, either. The bottom line is that we want different things."

His hand tightened on her elbow. "I want you in my life, Beth. After you left, I realized I missed you."

"Jonathan, I didn't leave." She stopped short of the camp and faced him. "You left me to go on another voluntary mission. Two weeks before our wedding." She shook her head. "I just made it more permanent by ending our engagement."

"I didn't want to end our engagement. I wanted to marry you."

"And I wanted a commitment. After you postponed our wedding for the second time, two weeks from the ceremony, I knew I would always come last."

He frowned. "I thought you, of all people, would understand. When we're called up...we go."

She smiled into his face. "I'm in the Army. I know what it means to see your loved ones leave. I know the Army has you first. Family is second. But there's a difference between being ordered to go and volunteering. You volunteered—two weeks before our wedding that had already been postponed."

"Volunteered?" For such an intelligent man, he looked like a confused child.

"Yes. You volunteered. They had other doctors who could have gone and let you make it through your wedding before you headed out again."

His lips pressed together. "So, it's the voluntary part of this puzzle that got to you?"

She nodded. "You volunteered to put me second in your life. I would've been disappointed but accepting if the deployment had been ordered. I expected that. The fact that you willingly put us on hold for the second time was what made me realize we weren't meant to be together."

He reached for her hands.

When she stepped back, he let his arms fall to his sides. "I can work on that."

"Why? This is what you do. This is your passion, more than any relationship you might have had with me."

"But we're good together."

"As a doctor and nurse. But as husband and wife, we'd fail miserably. I want more than you're capable of giving." She squared her shoulders and lifted her chin. "I did the right thing."

"Beth, I love you," he said. "I want to spend the rest of my life proving that to you. I wouldn't have asked you to marry me otherwise."

"Jonathan—" The sound of helicopter rotors pounding the air cut her off and made her turn toward the Black Hawk coming in for a landing. "Is it the Deltas coming back in?"

"Maybe."

A single soldier hopped off the craft and ran toward a group of men standing nearby.

Beth's pulse quickened when she recognized one of them as Doug Masters. Her core heated and a warm flush rose up her neck into her cheeks. "Let's go see what's happening."

As they hurried toward the men, the group broke up and ran toward their sleeping quarters.

The only man left standing on the edge of camp was the one who'd leaped out of the helicopter.

"What's happening?" Jonathan asked as they approached the Delta.

"We've run into a little trouble. The guys sent me back for reinforcements. You'll need to stand by for casualties. Have your flight medical team ready to go. The chopper will be back as soon as we drop off the fresh meat."

Beth flinched at his words. "Are our guys getting hit hard?"

"They weren't yet, but they were about to go into a village the Boko Haram are razing. They outnumber us at least four to one."

Beth's heart squeezed tightly in her chest. She almost asked if there was anything they could do to help but realized by being prepared to move as a medical team, they were doing what they could. She lifted her chin. "We'll be ready."

Dawg and his team came running, carrying

their weapons and extra magazines full of ammunition. They ran past Beth and Jonathan. Dawg cast a brief glance their way without breaking stride. They loaded onto the helicopter, along with the man from the other Delta team. The chopper's blades beat the air as the craft lifted off the ground and rose into the air. In a matter of seconds, it was gone, carrying men into danger.

Her breath hitched in her throat as the Black Hawk disappeared. Then she turned and ran with Jonathan back to the hospital tent to gather supplies and equipment they might need when the shooting stopped.

Beth's stomach knotted every time she thought about Dawg rushing into the fight. She hoped he'd keep his head down and come out of it intact. If this was what life as a Delta's woman was like…she wasn't sure she wanted any part of it. At this point, she didn't have a choice. She was there. Dawg was one of the men she'd been brought in to support. She had a job to do, and she needed to leave emotions out of it.

Yeah. Right. Like that would be easy.

THE PILOT BROUGHT the helicopter as close as he could to the hot zone and touched the ground long enough for the men to pile out onto the ground. The door gunner provided cover for the men on the ground as the chopper lifted into the air and flew out of range of small arms fire and any rocket-propelled grenades the terrorists might lob their way.

The men had their headsets tuned to the same frequency as the other Delta team already on the ground.

Every building in the small village was on fire. The villagers were scattering, running out into the underbrush. Some had been captured, herded into the center of the fires and forced to their knees.

"Glad you made it just in time. We need to stop them from executing those people," a voice said into Dawg's ear. "We've set up a perimeter halfway around the settlement. So far, they don't know how many of us are out here. As soon as we start taking out their men, all hell will break loose. The odds are four to one."

"Easy," Rucker said. "Let's do this before they kill those villagers."

"Got our best snipers ready. As soon as they pick off the assassins, we're moving forward."

"We've got your six," Rucker said.

Hunkering low, Dawg's team spread out and closed in on the village.

Gunfire was their cue.

The men holding the rifles to their captive's heads dropped to the ground.

The ones gathered around spun in their tracks and glanced toward the edge of the village.

Delta Force snipers dropped two more before the terrorists dove for the ground.

The villagers they'd captured scattered, heading for the cover.

Dawg moved into the village ahead of Mac, established himself at the corner of a building and waited for Mac to leapfrog to a position ahead of Dawg. He made it to the next corner and waved Dawg on.

Moving swiftly, he ran past Mac to the corner of a hut and peered around the edge. Several men carrying AK-47s ran toward him.

Dawg swung his rifle out in front of him, stepped out into the open and fired.

Three of the four men dropped. The fourth had time to raise his rifle.

A shot fired from behind Dawg nailed the bastard. He fell to the ground and lay still.

Mac and Dawg grabbed the terrorists' weapons, ejected the magazines and chambered rounds and slung the rifles into a burning hut before they moved on. Gunfire sounded all around them. The cries of villagers spurred Dawg on.

Dawg emerged near the center of the burning village as the other members of the team came out.

Trapped, the men of Boko Haram fired at anything that moved.

The villagers still around lay on the ground, either dead or too terrified to move.

Deltas fired, taking the men out, one by one, until the last three standing threw down their weapons and raised their hands in surrender. Bull, Mac and Blade hurried forward and secured the combatants.

The sun sank below the horizon, and the shadowy stillness of dusk settled over the burning village.

"Deltas sound off," Rucker's voice came across Dawg's headset. "Team Charlie."

One by one the members of Team Charlie sounded off. "Is that all of you?" Rucker asked.

"Yes, sir," a voice said. "Bodie took a hit to his left thigh."

"Team Bravo, sound off."

Mac nodded from his position near one of their prisoners. "Mac."

Dawg raised a hand. "Dawg."

Bull gave a chin lift as he stood over his prisoner. "Bull."

Blade straightened after applying a zip-tie to his prisoner's wrists. "Blade."

"Lance, on perimeter."

A long empty pause made Dawg's pulse quicken.

"Dash, sound off," Rucker said.

He was supposed to be on perimeter, too," Lance said.

"Sending Team Charlie out," a voice said.

Bull nodded toward Mac. "You got these guys?"

Mac nodded. "Go."

Rucker, Bull, Blade and Dawg spread out, heading for the perimeter of the village. The darker the sky got, the more worried Dawg became.

"Hey," a voice sounded in his headset. "Where'd everyone go?"

"Dash?" Rucker's voice came across. Where are you?"

"I'm not sure." Dash's voice sounded shaky.

"Can you stand?" Rucker asked.

"Don't know until I try," he said. A moment later he reported. "No can do. The world is tilting."

"If you can sit up, do it. We'll find you."

Dawg reached the edge of the village and lowered his night vision goggles. It was still a little too light outside, but he hoped he could pick up Dash's heat signature.

He scanned the corners of the buildings and swept his search out into the nearby tall grass. A light green lump appeared fifty yards from where Dawg stood. After checking for bogies, Dawg ran toward the heat signature.

When he arrived, he pushed the night vision goggles away from his eyes. "I found him," Dawg reported. "Hey, buddy, what happened to you?"

Dash shook his head. "I'm not exactly sure. One moment I was fine, the next moment, I was swimming." He moved to show a dark stain on the ground beneath him.

"Shit." Dawg dropped to his knees and ran his hands over Dash's leg. The blood was coming from the back of his thigh, and he was losing a lot of it. "Dash, I need to roll you over onto your stomach while I apply pressure to the wound."

"Roll away," Dash said, his voice weak. "I'd help you, but I think I'll sleep." He closed his eyes and lay his head on the ground.

Dawg rolled him over and pressed his hand to the wound.

By that time, Bull caught up with him. "Keep applying pressure," he said. As the team medic, he took over, pulling a thick wad of gauze from his stash in the pocket of his trousers. He folded the gauze into an even thicker pad. Then he moved Dawg's hand, pressing the gauze against the wound. "Now, hold that while I bind it in place." From the opposite pocket, he pulled out a roll of elastic bandage wrap and wound it around Dash's leg several times until he ran out of the roll.

The rest of Dawg's team gathered around Dash. Members of Team Charlie helped their wounded guy over to where Dash lay on his belly on the ground.

The thumping sound of a helicopter

approaching made Dawg feel more hopeful. The sooner they got Dash out of the grass and to the medical staff, the better.

Moments later, the chopper landed fifty yards from the village.

They'd be out of there soon, and Dash would get the care he desperately needed.

Across the field, a couple of men dropped down out of the helicopter. They unloaded a basket and carried it toward the men standing around Dash.

Colonel Parker and Beth brought up the rear, carrying what appeared to be medical tool kits.

The amount of relief Dawg felt at that moment made his knees weak. "Hang in there, Dash. The doc will have you up and running again in no time."

Dash didn't respond. He lay motionless on the ground, blood soaking through the bandage Bull had applied.

As soon as the medics arrived with the basket, Bull and Dawg helped get Dash into it.

Colonel Parker assessed the wound and had Beth start an IV of fluids. The medics, Bull and Dawg lifted the basket with Dash in it and carried it to the helicopter. Beth ran alongside them, holding the IV in the air.

They stowed Dash on the floor of the chopper and secured the basket. Colonel Parker had moved on to the other patient, performed a quick assessment and recommended he join them on the helicopter. The man from Team Charlie could walk with assistance and was able to be buckled into a harness, sitting up.

Dawg took Beth's hand and helped her up into the helicopter. As he let go, he looked up into her eyes. "Take care of Dash. He's family."

She nodded. "We'll do our very best."

A moment later, the helicopter lifted off with the two wounded Deltas, the doctor and Beth.

His heart racing, Dawg watched, praying some escaped member of the Boko Haram didn't shoot an RPG at the helicopter. That bird had two people who meant a lot to Dawg on board. Until he got word they were safe, he couldn't relax.

Putting the adrenaline to work, Dawg helped the villagers gather their wounded and dead.

The buildings were a total loss, and what few possessions they'd owned had been destroyed. The villagers would become like so many others, homeless and refugees in their own country.

Frightened children cried, and women wailed over the loss of loved ones.

Too often, Dawg felt overwhelmed at the horrible things man did to man in the name of religion.

Less than an hour later, the helicopter returned. Rucker insisted Team Charlie go back to camp in that round. The remaining Deltas set up a perimeter in case the terrorists returned. Darkness settled over the land with only the burning embers of the fires and the stars in the heavens lighting the sky.

Dawg prayed Dash hadn't lost too much blood. Not only was he a friend, he was his brother.

Thankfully, his brother was in good hands with Beth and Colonel Parker.

CHAPTER 8

"ARE ALL THE DELTAS BACK?" Beth asked Corporal Ramsey, who'd returned when the Black Hawk landed the second time.

He shook his head. "Team Bravo is still out there."

Beth's heart turned somersaults in her chest. "By themselves with no backup?"

"The helo is about to go back to get them after they fuel up. I'm going back with them. Are you coming, too?"

She nodded, making the decision in that instant. She just had to clear it with her commander.

Beth found Jonathan with Dash in the hospital. "How's he doing?"

"He'd going to be fine. Since we stopped the hemorrhaging, he's stabilized and the blood trans-fusion helped restore a little of what he lost."

"Are you good with the staff you have here?" she asked. "Do you need me?"

Jonathan looked up from the chart he'd been studying. "Of course, I need you."

She gritted her teeth and forced herself to remain calm. "I mean, do you need me now. I'd like to go back to the village and see if there's anything I can do to help." And she wanted to make certain Dawg was okay. Until she saw for herself, she couldn't relax.

"We can manage without you for a while. But are you sure you'll be safe?"

She nodded. "I'll take one of the medics. There's still a Delta team there, helping the villagers with the wounded. I think I could be of assistance."

Jonathan frowned. "I should come with you."

"One of us should stay with our wounded Deltas," Beth said. "Either you or me. I think it should be you in case you have to do emergency surgery on Dash."

"But the villagers might need me to help them."

"Our primary mission is to support the Deltas. If something happened to Dash while you were out helping villagers…" She trailed off.

Jonathan nodded. "I'll stay. You can do just about anything I can out there, short of invasive surgery. I just don't want anything to happen to you. Despite what you might think, I care a lot about you."

Beth smiled gently. "I know you do. I'll be okay. I'll stick close to the Deltas. They'll make sure I'm okay. But I need to go before the helicopter leaves." She grabbed a medical kit and raced out of the hospital and across the field to the waiting Black Hawk.

The pilot was just strapping himself into his seat when she climbed aboard and sat in the seat beside Corporal Ramsey. The gunner handed her a headset and buckled her harness for her. Moments later, the aircraft lifted off the ground and flew through the air. Before Beth could second guess her mad dash out to the besieged village, the chopper descended into the field beside the smoking buildings.

She climbed out of the helicopter, grabbed the medical kit and followed Ramsey through the maze of destroyed buildings.

Villagers were coming in a few at a time, searching through the rubble for their belongings or the food they'd stored.

Beth's heart hurt for them. These people had had so little to begin with, to lose even that was devastating.

She worked her way through the village, searching for Dawg. She found several of the Deltas helping the injured or assisting the people in their attempts to salvage what they could. She stopped to treat burns, cuts and busted lips. Ramsey assisted when she applied sutures to a man who'd cut his hand when he'd been thrown against a building. The people she helped were poor, desperate and grateful for anything she could do to make their lives easier.

All the while she helped the displaced people, she searched the faces of the Deltas for one. Had their one night together been enough to build a relationship on? Hell, had she called off her marriage because of Jonathan, or had she come to the conclusion he really wasn't the man for her? Did that make Dawg the right man for her? They'd only been out once and had made love twice. She couldn't fall in love with someone that quickly. It had to be lust.

Whatever it was, Beth was determined to find the man and make sure he was all right.

She was cleaning a scrape on a woman's arm when she spotted him helping a man bring bedding and clothing out of a smoldering building. He carried a flashlight and an armful of soot-covered belongings.

The man thanked him profusely for his help as he gathered his things and his family around him.

Dawg kneeled down in front of a little girl and spoke to her. Beth couldn't hear what he said, but the little girl grinned in the darkness, her teeth shining a bright white.

Beth's chest tightened. Though they'd lost so

much, they still had each other. The family had remained intact, thanks to the Deltas.

Beth had heard how Boko Haram terrorists had lined up many of the villagers, planning on killing them, execution style. And she' learned how the Delts had come to the rescue before that tragedy could take place.

On her way over to where Dawg still helped the man and his family, Beth stopped to check on a man lying on the ground.

He lay on the ground as still as death.

Beth leaned over him and pressed her fingers to the base of his neck, searching for a pulse. Just as she found it, his hand snapped up and gripped her wrist. He pressed a handgun to her temple, and he spoke crisply in English, "You will listen to me very carefully, or you will die."

"Seriously?" Her gut clenched.

"Do as I say, and I won't hurt you," he said.

"Okay," Beth said in her calmest tone though she was shaking inside. "What do you want?"

"I want out of here," he said. "Alive."

"And how do you propose to do that?" she asked.

"If anyone comes close, you will tell them to back away. You will walk with me to the edge of the village as if I were any other villager. Now, help me to my feet. One wrong move, and I will kill you."

"You do realize that if you kill me, they will kill you?" she said.

"But you will die first." He tapped her temple with the barrel of the weapon. "Do you wish to risk it?"

She sighed. "No."

With the gun in his hand pressed to her temple, he pulled his feet beneath him and lurched to a standing position, leaning heavily on one leg.

For a brief moment, the gun slipped from the position against her temple. Beth bunched her muscles, ready to spring away from the man and his threats. But the barrel of the pistol pressed to her temple again, reminding her of the finality of a bullet to the brain.

Once the man was steady on his feet, he moved the gun to point it at her side, half-hidden from view by her body. "Now, walk," he said.

Beth moved toward the edge of the village, careful not to jostle the man and his gun. She wanted to live to see another day back in the States where she had a date with a handsome Delta.

Though he moved with a limp, he set off with purpose, heading away from the people congregating around the center of the village. As they neared the outskirts of the village, a shout sounded behind them.

"Beth?"

Her heart skipped several beats at the sound of Dawg's voice behind her.

"Keep moving," the man beside her said, jabbing her in the ribs with the hard metal of the handgun.

She winced as pain shot through her. Still, she kept moving.

Dawg would realize soon that she wasn't going of her own accord, and he'd come to her rescue.

"Beth?" he called out again. "Wait up."

Beth ignored him again, getting closer to the edge of town. Though she wanted to be rescued, she was afraid her captor would try to shoot Dawg.

Dawg followed, closing the distance between them a little at a time. "Beth, wait."

When Beth and her captor reached the edge of the village, Beth ground to a halt. "I got you this far, you can make it on your own now."

"Not without you. You're my ticket to freedom."

"Look, I've got too many people waiting for me to help them. You can make your escape without me."

He pressed the gun into her side. "Or you can die now."

Anger rippled through her. This man was one of the men who'd destroyed the village. She'd gotten him this far. But to let him walk away from the devastation without any resistance wasn't right. Not after what he'd done to the innocent people of the village.

"Go on. Keep moving," he said, his tone firm, his hand unwavering on the gun.

"No." Beth stood her ground, praying the man didn't fulfill his promise to kill her. "Go ahead, run into the brush. I'm not going with you. And if you don't go soon, I'll yell and alert the villagers that you're among them. Without the rest of your friends, you are nothing. They will kill you in a slow, painful death." She tipped her head back toward the village. "And that man following us is a trained killer. He's coming for me. You only have seconds to make up your mind." She glanced over her shoulder at the silhouette of Dawg moving toward them in the darkness.

The man looked too, giving Beth the opportunity she'd been waiting for.

She shoved him hard and dove to the ground, rolling to one side.

The terrorist stumbled, the injury on his leg making movement awkward. Then he took off, running into the brush and darkness.

A moment later, Dawg caught up with Beth. "Are you all right?" he asked, pulling her into his arms.

She nodded and pressed her cheek to his chest, so very glad they were alone and away from prying eyes. Her body shook, and tears filled her eyes. "He told me was going to shoot me."

"Th man you were with a second ago?"

She nodded. "He was one of Boko Haram. He wanted me to go with him as his ticket to escape."

He held her at arms' length and stared down into her eyes, his own eyes reflecting the starlight. "How did you get away?"

"I told him I wasn't going with him, and that the man behind me was a trained killer. When he looked, back, I shoved him hard. He took off."

"That's too bad he got away. But then I'd rather he get away than put a bullet in you." Again, he crushed her in his arms and pressed his lips to hers.

The same electric current she'd felt with him back in Texas rippled through her, making her want to hold him tighter, to lie with him naked and make love with him through the night and into the morning. But they were in enemy territory. Not to mention, they couldn't act on their feelings. Not in theater. They could both be court-marshalled and kicked out of the military. Whatever they were feeling had to stay on the down low until they returned to the States.

But it felt so good to be held. And what would it hurt to steal one kiss?

Beth tipped up her chin. "I know this is wrong, but I want to do this. No...I need to do this." She pushed up on her toes and brushed her lips across his.

He crushed her in his arms and returned the kiss with a searing one of his own, claiming her tongue and holding her like there might be no tomorrow.

When, at last, they came up for air, Beth laid her cheek against his chest. "We should get back to the others before they come looking for us."

He nodded and smoothed the hair back from her forehead before pressing a light kiss there. "I don't know if I'll be able to keep my hands off you for the duration of this deployment."

She wrapped her arms around his waist, hugged him hard then stepped away. "We have to. We can't let this ruin our careers. We've both worked too hard for what we have. I refuse to let you get thrown out of the Army, and I won't leave unless it's on my own terms. Come on. The helicopter pilot didn't want us to stay too long,"

Dawg captured her hand and brought it up to his lips. "At least we have something to look forward to when we get back home." He brushed his lips across the back of her knuckles and released her.

They walked back to the center of the village together where they found the rest of Dawg's team preparing to leave.

Beth found Corporal Ramsey and collected the medical kit. The helicopter landed, the pilot waiting for the Deltas and the medical staff to climb on board. They loaded quickly. Every second they were on the ground was an opportunity for the enemy to fire on them.

Once everyone was accounted for, the Black Hawk lifted off the ground and flew back to their base.

Beth was glad she'd gone, even if she'd almost been kidnapped to shield a terrorist during his escape. Dawg had hugged and kissed her like he really did like her and want to be with her. The spark was still there, giving her hope for the future. A future that might see her settling down with a Delta.

After checking her patients, Beth headed for her quarters, peeled off half of her clothes and laid down on her cot, enjoying the cool night air. She lay there for a long time, thinking about Dawg, about Jonathan and about her career. The more time she spent with Dawg the more she liked him.

Was it love?

Maybe.

She hoped they would have the opportunity to find out.

CHAPTER 9

DAWG HANDED Beth out of the helicopter, knowing how exhausting the night had been. She stumbled and would have fallen if he hadn't been there to help steady her. Together, they walked toward the camp.

Dr. Parker was waiting for them as the team ducked beneath the camouflage netting. Some of his teammates made a beeline for the shower facility.

Since Beth stopped in front of Dr. Parker, Dawg did, too.

"Any more casualties?" the doctor asked.

Beth shook her head. "No, sir."

The man's eyes narrowed as he studied Beth. "Are you all right?"

She nodded, her cheeks flooding with color. "I

just need a shower and a good night's sleep. Are our patients resting easily?"

The doctor nodded. "No complications, thus far."

"That's good. I'll check in on them in the morning." Beth smothered a yawn. "Right now, I'm way beyond tired."

"Don't let me stand between a woman and her bed," Dawg said with a grin.

Jonathan's brow furrowed as he watched her walk away. "Can I buy you a cup of coffee?"

Dawg was tired and wanted to hit the shower then bed. He smelled of smoke from helping villagers salvage belongings from their damaged homes. But he also wanted to know why the good doctor wanted to speak with him. "Sure."

They walked to the dining area where a coffeepot was kept with a healthy amount of coffee grinds for those in the military to enjoy.

A carafe of coffee was already on the burner keeping warm.

Dr. Parker pulled out two cups from his cabinet and set them on the counter near the coffeemaker. He poured coffee into the two cups and set them on a table.

Dawg sat in front of one of the cups and lifted it to his lips.

Jonathan dropped onto the seat opposite Dawg and launched into the discussion. "I sense something happening between you and Lieutenant Drennan."

Dawg tensed. He hadn't expected the doctor to say anything like that, and frankly, he didn't know what to say in response. "Excuse me?" he said to buy time while he digested the topic of the doctor's conversation. "There's nothing going on between the lieutenant and me. That would be against policy."

The doctor nodded. "Precisely. Fraternizing while deployed can get you an Article 15, or worse, court-martialed."

Dawg nodded. "I know the regs."

"Good. I'd hate to see either one of you lose your careers because you didn't know the rules."

"I appreciate your concern, but there's nothing going on between me and the lieutenant," Dawg repeated.

"Even if we weren't in theater, Army regs discourage relationships between officers and enlisted." Dr. Parker gave Dawg a pointed stare.

Dawg dipped his head once. "I understand."

"You both have very promising military careers," the doctor continued.

Dawg set his cup aside, tired of the man beating around the bush. "Is there something you want to get off your chest, sir?"

Parker sighed. "I want the lieutenant to be happy, no matter who she chooses to spend her life with. She's a special, giving person, who needs someone who can provide for her the life she so richly deserves."

"I admit, I like the lieutenant," Dawg said. "And I agree, she deserves happiness. But she has to make that determination of what makes her happy."

"Or who." Dr. Parker met Dawg's gaze, his eyes narrowing.

"She would be the best judge of the who." Dawg sat up straighter and wrapped his hand around his cup. "Sir, is that all you wanted to discuss?"

The doctor nodded. "It is. Your team did an admirable job tonight against overwhelming odds."

"How's Dash?" Dawg asked.

"He's recovering nicely. We need to get him back to the States soon, so he can get his physical therapy started."

"Thank you for taking care of him. My team is my family."

"You need to make sure that's not all the family you need. Your job takes you away a great deal of the time. It's not much of a life for those left behind."

Dawg's lips curled slightly. "That's so very true. It's a major consideration in any relationship. But I've seen it work for some of my friends. It's how you love your family when you're with them that makes the difference."

"Sometimes, even that isn't enough when the

distance and time are too great." Dr. Parker pushed to his feet. "Get some rest, Sergeant."

Dawg rose from his seat. "Yes, sir."

The two men parted ways.

Dawg walked away from the camp, just far enough to get out from under the canopy so that he could see the stars.

Everything Parker had mentioned had gone through his mind on numerous occasions, leaving him with the same question...*was he the right person for Beth?*

Beth was an amazing nurse and a wonderful human. She cared about people and her friends.

And she was an incredible lover, full of passion and warmth.

If he truly cherished her, he'd want only the best for Beth. Was being married to the doctor the best thing for Beth?

He was an officer. That would keep things straight so far as the military was concerned. The man was brilliant as a physician and surgeon, according to what the medics and locals had to say. But was he as good at relationships as Beth wanted and needed?

Dawg was convinced he and Beth would be good together. They were both passionate in bed, but also about their work. Yet, when they were together, they were totally focused on each other, not the next mission or patient. That's what she'd needed from her doctor-fiancé.

Had Dr. Parker come to his senses since losing Beth? Would he give her what she needed?

Should Dawg step back and let them figure it out without him interfering and adding to the confusion?

He shoved a hand through his hair and decided all decisions could wait until after he'd had a shower and a good night's sleep.

One thing was certain, when he'd seen Beth held at gunpoint by the Boko Haram terrorist, he would've moved heaven and earth, and sacrificed his own life, to save her. Though they'd only been together for a short time, they'd discovered they had so much in common and had bonded over dogs.

So, they weren't both in the medical field, and they both were deployed often. They at least knew what it meant to be a part of the military and understood they had signed up for that lifestyle.

The difference between Dawg and Dr. Parker was that Dawg knew when to focus on family over another potentially exciting assignment. If he'd had the choice between volunteering for another deployment or marrying Beth, he would've chosen marrying Beth. No question.

Dawg headed for his tent, grabbed his toiletries

and hurried to the shower facility, which wasn't much more than another tent with a single pipe connected to a water tank. The trickle of water and a bar of soap was enough to wash the dust and camouflage paint from his skin. He rinsed, dried off and slipped into PT shorts. When he stepped out of the shower tent, he almost ran into someone about to enter. He gripped that person's arms to keep from bowling him over.

"Dawg," a familiar voice said in the dark.

Beth.

His hands tightened on her arms. "Hey."

"Hey," she echoed.

The conversation he'd had with Dr. Parker rushed back into his mind. Dawg dropped his hands from her arms. "Going for a shower?"

She wore a robe, flipflops and carried a towel and her toiletries. "I'm hoping it will help me relax."

He snorted. "That cold dribble of water? I doubt seriously it will relax you."

"Well, being clean would go a long way toward making me feel better." She looked up into his eyes. Starlight reflected off her irises. "You might be used to being shot at or held at gunpoint, but that was a first for me."

"It might be a while before you get over it. Some never do."

She nodded. "PTSD." Beth reached out and touched his arm. "About earlier…"

"I shouldn't have kissed you." Dawg jumped in

with everything Parker had said still weighing heavily on his mind.

Beth laughed. "I thought I was the one kissing *you*. But that wasn't what I was going to say."

Dawg frowned. "I meant I think it's a bad idea to kiss while we're deployed."

"I was going to say thank you," Beth said. "For being there when I needed you. And you're right. We shouldn't have. And I shouldn't have initiated it." She held up a hand as if swearing in court. "I promise not to initiate a kiss until we get back stateside." Her smile lit the night, making Dawg's heart pound harder.

"Do you want me to stay until you're done?" he asked.

"That won't be necessary," Beth said. "You need to get some sleep. I'm headed that direction after my shower." She turned toward the tent, stopped and turned back. "For the record, that kiss was every bit as good as the ones back in Texas. I don't regret it in the least. It was totally worth the risk." Then she ducked into the tent, leaving Dawg outside with his pulse pounding and with the urge to follow her into the tent, strip her naked and make love to her there in trickling, cold water.

He drew in a long, slow breath, held it and let it out in an attempt to get a grip on his desire.

Dawg wanted Beth to be happy. If it meant her going back to her doctor ex-fiancé, he'd be gracious and glad for her. But he'd be sad for himself. If he wasn't already there, he was well on his way to falling in love with the pretty lieutenant. If he followed his heart, he'd pull out all the stops and woo her properly. But to truly love her, he had to do what was right for her. Dawg wasn't sure he was her Mr. Right.

BETH SPENT the next day taking care of their Special Forces patients and getting them ready to be airlifted to Landstuhl, Germany. Dash was already feeling better. The blood transfusion had helped to restore some of his energy. Time would take care of the rest.

The afternoon in the village hospital took even longer that day with folks coming to them from the village destroyed by Boko Haram the night before. The Special Forces guys went out to help salvage what they could and start the cleanup effort. Not all the villagers returned to rebuild. Some ended up in the temporary refugee camp that was becoming more permanent by the day.

By the end of the day, Beth was hungry and ready to put up her feet up and relax.

After one last check on the men in the Army field hospital, Beth emerged from the tent and stretched the kinks out of her back. She would never get used to sleeping on an Army cot. Not when her bed back in Texas was so soft and her feather pillow just perfect for shaping into anything form she desired.

With visions of food and sleep foremost in her mind, she turned toward her quarters only to be waylaid when a tall, dark-haired man stepped into her path.

Beth screeched to a halt and threw up her hands. "Geez, Dawg, you scared the crap out of me."

"Sorry," he said. "I wanted to catch you before you disappeared. Would you like to have dinner with me tonight?"

She frowned. "I thought we agreed not to see each other while deployed."

"We agreed not to kiss and demonstrate any public displays of affection. But we still have to eat, so why not do it together? Besides, we need to talk."

Beth's frown deepened. She didn't like the sound of his words. *We have to talk* didn't bode well. It sounded like when she'd had *the breakup talk* with Jonathan. Her heart stuttered a few beats, and then kicked into high speed. They'd barely started going out when they'd deployed. Were the deployment and rank issues already getting to him? She hoped not.

The more she was with Dawg, the more she wanted to be with him.

"Okay," she said. "When?"

"I'm ready now." He held up two packages of MREs and two bottles of water. "I'm buying."

She laughed. "I guess now is good." Beth didn't like lingering doubt. She was a proponent for ripping the bandage off, rather than prolonging the anticipation of pain.

When he turned away from the dining area, she had to hurry to catch up with him. "Where are we going?"

"To watch the sunset," he said and led her to the western end of the Army camp where an Army green wool blanket lay on the ground, held down by several large rocks.

"You planned ahead," Beth noted. "All we need now is wine."

"And decent food," Dawg added. "Have a seat. Your dinner will be served momentarily." He pulled a knife out of the scabbard at his hip and tore into one of the packets. "You have a choice between barbecue and beef stew."

"I'll take the barbecue." She probably wouldn't eat much of it. Not if it meant delaying *the talk*. Her stomach would roil until he told her they were breaking it off. But then she could deal with it. Not knowing was the worst kind of pain.

"Good choice," Dawg said, as if nothing in the world was wrong. Damn him for being so calm and collected when Beth's world could potentially fall apart at any moment. She didn't want things to end between them. Not now, or ever. They were perfect for each other. Or at least, she hoped they were.

They ate, talking about what had happened the night before and what could happen again since they'd stirred up the hornet's nest by interfering with the activities of the Boko Haram.

Though she tried to act normal, Beth's nerves stretched with each passing minute.

After they put away the trash into one of the empty packets, they stretched out to watch the sun dip below the horizon, a glorious ball of fire melting into the earth.

"So, what is it you really wanted to talk about?" she finally asked.

He stared at the horizon turning gray without the brightness of the sun. "I think you need to give Colonel Parker a second chance."

Beth's eyebrows shot upward. "What?"

Dawg sighed. "There had to be something there when you agreed to marry him. He regrets having volunteered for an assignment so close to the wedding. He knows what he did wrong, and he loves you."

Beth shook her head slowly and shifted her gaze from Dawg to the horizon. "So, now you're a marriage counselor?" She laughed. "Is this your way of dumping me? Because you don't have to go through throwing my ex back at me. I can walk away, if that's what you want."

Dawg shoved a hand through his hair, making it stand on end. It also made him look even more adorable, which only made Beth angrier.

"I don't want to dump you," he said. "I like your company. We have so much in common, and I've never wanted to kiss a woman more."

She crossed her arms over her chest and pinned him with her gaze. "I hear a *but* coming."

He shrugged. "But it wouldn't be right for me to come between you and your former fiancé. He still has feelings for you."

"And what I want doesn't count?" She challenged him with a glare.

"Absolutely. Colonel Parker made some good points, though."

"Like?"

"Like, a relationship between the two of us would be difficult in the eyes of the Army, with you being an officer and me being enlisted."

Her brow descended. "Did he threaten you?"

Dawg held up both hands. "No. Not at all. He just made some valid points."

"What were the others?" she demanded, getting madder by the minute. How dare her ex-fiancé warn off another man?

"He knows how often Deltas get deployed," Dawg said. "I'd be gone more than your doctor ever will be."

"I never said I had a problem with him being

gone. I had a problem that he chose to be gone over marrying me." She shook her head. "Look, are you dumping me or not? I'd like to know if I'll have a date when we get back Stateside."

Dawg grinned. "If you decide not to go back to your ex, we'll definitely have a date. If I haven't screwed us up with this conversation."

She narrowed her eyes. "I make my own decisions. No amount of pushing me in a certain direction will make me change my mind. Either you want to be with me, or you don't. If you really want me to be with my ex, then I'll assume you don't want to be with me."

Dawg's grin broadened. "For the record, and for my own selfish reasons, I don't want you to be with your ex. I want you to be happy. That's all."

"Then let me decide what will make me happy." She sucked in a deep breath and huffed it out. "Now, if you'll excuse me, I'm mad, and I don't want to take it out on you." She stood, brushed the dust off her uniform and tipped her head toward the horizon. "Thanks for the food and the sunset. Next time, stop at that. I'm not going back to Jonathan."

"He's a good guy," Dawg said. "I wish he wasn't."

"I know that," Beth said. that fact had made it harder to end their engagement, because he is a good guy. "That's not why I broke up with him. We want different things. That's all." She stared across

ELLE JAMES

the space between them, feeling like it was more than just inches.

Dawg reached for her but stopped when his hands were halfway there and let them drop back to his sides. "I want to hold you, to kiss you and reassure you that I'm not dumping you. I want to get to know you better, and mostly, I want you to be happy."

"If Colonel Parker is warning you off me, we'd better keep our interactions on the up and up. Good night, Sergeant Masters."

"Good night, Lieutenant Drennan."

She wanted to say more but couldn't. Not when her career could be at stake. If Jonathan suspected she and Dawg were having an affair, he could end their careers. She hoped that the man had enough feelings left for her that he wouldn't. But that didn't mean he wouldn't make Dawg's career a mess. Again, Beth didn't think Jonathan would do that... but she couldn't risk it. With a silent sigh, she turned and walked away. It was the only thing she could do.

CHAPTER 10

Dawg gathered the trash, the wool blanket and his tattered ego.

Beth had been right. She was the one who held all the cards. It was her decision which man she would choose. Dawg was just sorry he'd started the conversation in the first place. They'd been doing well without him trying to push her back toward the good doctor.

He stopped at the dining area, dumped his trash and continued on to his sleeping quarters.

As he approached the tents assigned to his team, he noticed Rucker standing outside in the starlight holding a satellite phone to his ear. He ended the call as Dawg reached him and shook his head. "Looks like another busy night. Get the team together; Boko Haram is at it again. Our intelligence sources report another village being attacked nearby. The powers that be want us to get out there, find Kahbir and take care of him like we should have when we took out his commander."

"I'll roust the others," Dawg said

"Not necessary." Mac poked his head out of a tent. "We're up and moving. We'll be ready in five minutes."

Blade stuck his head out of the tent Dawg shared with him. "Heard you. We're on it."

"Helo is on the way. It'll be here in ten minutes," Rucker informed them. "Looks like another night like before."

"Are we taking Team Charlie?"

Rucker nodded. "While we have them, we are."

Dawg nodded. "I'll let them know."

Rucker ducked into his tent to gather his gear.

Dawg raced to where the other team was quartered and let their lead know what was happening. He assured Dawg they'd be there when the helicopter landed.

"Those bastards don't give up, do they?" Dawg commented.

Team Charlie's leader pressed his lips together. "No. They don't. Comes from being religious zealots. They think their way is the only way."

Dawg raced back to his tent, grabbed his body armor and loaded up with his weapons and ammunition, communications device and his helmet equipped with night vision goggles. He did a quick mental check off of everything he'd need, then ran with the others of his team to where two Black Hawk helicopters were landing.

Team Charlie arrived at the same time, and they loaded into the first aircraft. Within less than three minutes, both teams were on their way.

As they left the ground, Dawg looked back at the village with the camp hidden beneath the desert camouflage netting. Somewhere down there, Beth was steaming mad about his stumbling attempts to make sure she was making the right decision for herself. He hated leaving her when she was angry and hated more that he hadn't been able to hold her in his arms before she'd walked away. He'd learned early on in his career as a Delta Force operator, that you don't leave things undone. You never knew if you'd make it back to finish it or make it right. He'd witnessed the fallout of life's moments left undone. Those left behind were filled with regret that ate at them for years to come.

He sighed and pulled his focus back into the present and the operation ahead. They had to take Kahbir out if he was there, orchestrating this raid. The man was equally as evil and destructive as his predecessor and needed to be eliminated.

As they neared the coordinates of the village, the helicopter slowed and lowered to land in a clearing just short of a ridge. The pilot explained that on the other side of the ridge was the small village which was currently being ransacked. They'd have to go in on foot to retain some element of surprise.

The two teams leaped out of the choppers and set off across the hill, dropping down to the village on the other side.

There, they found the Boko Haram raising hell, killing and burning much like they had the night before, only not on as big a scale as they had. In fact, there was less than a quarter of the terrorists creating the carnage.

It didn't take long for the Deltas to bring them under control, capturing several of the terrorists alive for the intel people to interrogate.

One of the young terrorists laughed and spit in Dawg's face. "You Americans are like sheep to be led."

Dawg fought the urge to plant his fist in the man's mouth. Instead, he calmly wiped the spittle from his cheek and cocked a brow. "Why do you say that?"

The terrorist's lips curled in an evil smile. "Why are there so few of us and so many of you here?" he said, answering a question with a question.

Dawg's eyes narrowed. Why indeed were there more Americans handling a small outbreak. Intelligence reports had been wrong. But if the Boko Haram combatants weren't all where Intel had sent them, where else would they go?"

As soon as the question came to Dawg's mind, the answer followed with chilling speed. He ran to Rucker who stood on the edge of village supervising the collection of prisoners and any data that might be useful in locating and eliminating more of the radical group.

"Call in the choppers," Dawg demanded.

"I will, when we're ready," Rucker said. "Why do you want them now?"

He tipped his head toward the small village. "The bulk of Boko Haram isn't here. One of the guys we captured laughed in my face and said the reason this smaller group was here was to draw the Deltas so the majority of their force could stage a secret attack somewhere else."

Rucker's gaze met Dawg's. "The camp."

Dawg nodded while his gut twisted into a hard knot. "Can you get word to the folks left behind?"

Rucker powered on the satellite phone and called the camp. Several rings later, one of the medics answered.

Rucker didn't wait for pleasantries. "Boko Haram is on its way to the village and the camp. Evacuate immediately all personnel."

"How soon until the Black Hawks land?" Dawg asked.

Rucker got back on the radio with the helicopter pilots, posing the same question. He thanked whoever had answered and turned to Dawg. "Five minutes." Then he yelled to the others standing nearby. "Wheels up in five!"

The teams wrapped up what they could and positioned themselves near the landing zone.

As soon as the choppers touched down, the men climbed into the helicopters. The birds lifted off the ground and sped away from the village to land near the one beside the hospital and medical staff, including Beth.

Dawg prayed they weren't too late.

BETH HAD GONE BACK to her tent with full intentions of going to bed and catching up on her sleep. When she got there, she found PFC Miller coming out of her tent, a frown denting his forehead.

"PFC Miller, are you looking for me?" she asked.

He looked up to find her striding toward him and grinned. "Yes, ma'am. Colonel Parker needs you in the tent with the detained combatants ASAP."

"Is one of them bleeding again?" she asked as she fell in step with the young private.

"I'm not sure. Intelligence folks showed up a few minutes ago. They want medical staff present in case one of the prisoners has a medical condition that could interfere with their interrogation."

"Gotcha." She ducked into the tent where the

prisoners had been held until the military intelligence team could retrieve them and question them on the movements of the Boko Haram.

Jonathan was already there. One of the prisoners had been seated in a chair, his hands secured behind him with a zip-tie.

The military intelligence representative questioned him in English. "Where is your base of operations?"

The man shook his head, staring down at his lap with his entire body shaking.

Beth wondered if the intel guys had roughed him up, but she didn't see any signs of bruises or blood. The man was obviously frightened of something.

"Tell us where it is, and we'll let you go."

He shook his head. "They will kill us if we tell." He looked around, his eyes wide and afraid. "They will kill us anyway. They will think we told. They will kill us when they come."

"When they come?" The interrogator leaned forward. "What do you mean *when they come?*"

The man trembled, and tears formed in his eyes. "They will kill us, and they will kill everyone here." He looked into the interrogator's eyes. "Please. Let us go. We will leave and run as fast as we can. Please...let us go."

"Is the Boko Haram coming here to the camp?" the interrogator asked.

The man in the chair nodded.

"When?"

"Soon."

"How soon?" the military intelligence guy persisted.

"Very soon."

Corporal Ramsey appeared in the doorway of the tent, holding a satellite phone in his hand, his eyes wide, his face white. "The Delta Force teams are on their way back. They said we're about to come under attack by the Boko Haram. We're to evacuate the camp, ASAP."

The prisoner sobbed. "Please. Let us go."

Jonathan leaped to his feet. "We have to get the patients out. Ramsey, I'll need you and PFC Miller to help me get our two Deltas out of the hospital and into the ambulances and away from here. Someone needs to warn the villagers."

"I'll go," Beth said.

Jonathan frowned. "No, find someone else. I need you with me to work with our patients."

"I'll be back quickly. It's not that far." Beth was already out the door and running toward the village when trucks rolled into view between her and the mud and stick huts.

"They're here!" she yelled and altered her direction for the hospital tent. They had to get the Deltas out and away before the terrorists found them and used them as examples of what they would do to people who opposed them.

"Everyone out!" she yelled. "Run for the brush, hide."

The three local women who helped with cleaning ran out of the tent.

Jonathan, Miller and Ramsey entered the tent. Miller and Ramsey scooped Dash up between them and left through the rear of the tent, heading for the ambulance at the far end of the compound.

An explosion shook the ground beneath Beth, and gunfire sounded much too close for comfort.

Jonathan hooked his arm around the Team Charlie patient and led him to the back exit of the hospital tent. "Get out, Beth."

"I'm coming." Knowing how precious antibiotics were, she hurried to the lock box where the vials were stored and shoved the key into the lock. Her hand shook so hard she almost couldn't turn the key. When the box finally opened, she scooped as many of the vials and pills as she could into her pockets. Shouts outside the tent made her abandon the rest and race for the back exit.

Beth made it through the tent flap and out into the open, heading for the field surrounding the camp. She'd made it to the edge of the camouflage canopy when she was hit from behind and tackled to the ground.

She fought, kicking and screaming, but the man

on top of her was much heavier and effortlessly held her pinned.

More men in black outfits with black turbans wrapped around their heads surrounded her. They bound her wrists with duct tape. The man who'd originally tackled her slung her over his shoulder and carried her to a truck, tossing her into the back. With her arms rendered immobile, she was unable to break her fall. Her head hit the hard metal and everything went black.

CHAPTER 11

BY THE TIME the Deltas returned, the Army camp and the village were in flames.

Dawg's heart sank to his knees as he leaped out of the helicopter onto the ground and ran toward what was left of the tents and the camouflage canopy.

Villagers stumbled out of the grass and under-brush, tears in their eyes as they surveyed what was left of their homes.

Dawg's hopes lifted when he spotted PFC Miller and Corporal Ramsey with Dash's arms looped over their shoulders, emerging from a nearby field. He ran toward them, his gaze sweeping the field for more of the military personnel who'd kept the small tent city running. Several soldiers came out of hiding, helping older villagers. One of the villagers who'd worked with the US military assisted the wounded Team Charlie Delta from his hiding place in the brush.

As others emerged and the smoke cleared, it became clear. Beth and Colonel Parker were gone.

Rucker got on the satellite phone and asked for assistance locating the missing doctor and nurse while Dawg paced, feeling useless in the wake of the attack.

"That's excellent news," Rucker was saying. "We're loading up now. I'll relay the coordinates to the pilot." He ended the call. "Our guys at Langley are on top of it. They've been conducting satellite surveillance in the area since we landed, trying to nail the location of the Boko Haram base. They've been moving at least once every three or four days."

"How is that going to help us if they've been moving?" Dawg demanded. "We need to know where they've taken Lieutenant Drennan and Colonel Parker now. Today."

Rucker held up a hand. "Fortunately, they had their satellites trained on our position when the terrorists struck. They were able to follow them to their current base. But they say it appears they are preparing to bug out. We have to get there before that happens. Gather the teams."

Dawg was running before the last words left Rucker's mouth.

Within minutes, they had the Deltas loaded into the helicopter and were lifting off the ground. They swung east, heading in the direction the men at Langley had indicated.

They rode with the doors open, the wind whipping through, making the heat more bearable. Dawg had chosen a seat on the outside edge of the helicopter. He stared down at the darkened landscape, straining his eyes to see more, to find Beth before Boko Haram did horrible things to her. Hopefully, they would keep her alive and well in order to ransom her and the doctor for money. However, with them being US citizens and members of the military, the terrorists might decide to kill them as an example to others.

Dawg couldn't let himself think that way. If they'd decided to kill them, they would've done it already and left their bodies in the ashes of the village. The fact that they'd taken only the doctor and the nurse could mean they had need of medical assistance, and then they might ransom them later.

Either way, the Deltas were going to get them back.

Alive.

BETH WOKE several minutes after she'd passed out in the back of the truck and wished she'd remained unconscious. Every time they hit a rut in the dirt road, her head hit the metal floor of the truck bed, making her head hurt. She pushed her way into a sitting position, propping herself up against another body lying beside her. In the light from the stars above, she could see the body belonged to Jonathan.

Her heart lodged in her throat. He lay so still. Was he dead? With her wrists secured behind her back, she couldn't reach out to press her fingers to the base of his neck to feel for a pulse. Instead, she scooted around to touch her fingers to the inside of his wrist, also secured behind his back. It was difficult to feel anything with the truck bumping along. After a few minutes, she gave up.

Then Jonathan moved, his arms twitching and his legs pushing outward. The terrorists had secured his ankles but hadn't secured hers. Somehow, she had to break the duct tape free around her wrists and figure out a way to escape. She couldn't just roll out of the back of the truck because there were four other men seated on the sides, armed with AK-47s. Even if she managed to roll out and not die from the fall, they would plug her so full of bullets, and she wouldn't survive anyway.

Until the odds improved, she was stuck in the back of the truck.

Several more jarring bumps later, Jonathan came to and pushed to a sitting position.

The four men aimed their AK-47s at him as a show of force.

Jonathan shook his head and looked around.

When he spied Beth, his shook his head. "I told you to run," he whispered.

She gave him a weak smile. "I didn't want them to steal the antibiotics. That stuff is like gold around here."

"Are you okay?" he asked, his brow furrowed.

She nodded. "And you?"

"I am, though my head's a little fuzzy."

The truck slowed as it climbed into the hills and eventually came to a halt.

The man surrounding Beth and Jonathan leaped out, then reached in and dragged their captives out and onto their feet. One of the men jabbed a knife through the bindings around Jonathan's ankles allowing him to kick free of the tape.

With AK-47's poking them in their backs, Beth and Jonathan were marched across a compound and pushed into a hut made of sheets of tin kluged together with wire and screws. The door was closed, throwing them into pitch darkness.

Immediately, Beth moved around the tiny space, searching for a rough surface, which wasn't hard to find. "Jonathan, find a rough surface and rub the tape against the metal. We have to break through the tape and find our way out of here."

She was working on getting the tape free when their captors returned, grabbed Jonathan and hauled him out of the hut.

"No!" Beth cried and tried to stop them.

One of the men slammed the butt of his rifle into her gut, knocking her down. The door shut behind him, and Beth was alone.

With the wind knocked out of her, she sat for a moment fighting back the tears. What were they going to do to Jonathan? She didn't want to marry him, but she didn't wish him dead.

Once she could breathe normally again, she went to work, rubbing the tape against a jagged piece of metal. Before long, she broke through several layers of the tape until the last piece snapped, and she pulled her wrists apart. Removing the duct tape took a layer of skin with it, but her hands were free.

Beth felt her way around the tin hut, returning to the door that was nothing more than a sheet of tin secured by wire hinges. She could see through the cracks to where a guard stood outside. If he would walk away, she might ease through the opening and sneak way without him knowing. She needed a distraction.

Dropping to her knees, she felt along the dirt floor, hoping to find a rock, stick or something she could shove through the crack in the door to make a noise.

She didn't have to. Shouts sounded, and men ran past the hut.

Her guard called out to the men running past, and then he took off after them.

Beth pushed against the door only to discover it had been secured by a wire tied to a nail on the other side. She pushed harder, stretching the wire as far as she could, creating a gap barely wide enough for a child to get through. But she bent, contorted and squeezed through the gap, ripping her shirt and her skin before she fell out on the ground. She rolled to her feet and ducked behind the tin hut.

She could have run and saved herself, but she couldn't leave without Jonathan.

Moving between huts, tents and barrels, she worked her way through the compound.

Men ran, throwing equipment and supplies into the backs of trucks, shouting to each other as they went. No one seemed to see Beth as she slipped through broken pallets, cardboard boxes, crates and junk littering the ground.

Ahead, what appeared to be an old army tent stood in the middle of the compound. Several guards carrying AK-47s surrounded it, guarding what was inside. If they'd taken Jonathan anywhere, it had to be inside that tent. The other structures were in the process of being torn down and loaded into the backs of the trucks.

Beth circled wide of the main tent, looking for a side that wasn't as heavily guarded. The rear of the tent had only one man guarding it, but there wasn't a door flap there.

If she could get close enough, she might distract the guard and slip beneath the bottom edge of the tent to see what was inside. She prayed for another distraction that would coax the guard into running away.

As if in answer to her silent prayer, one of the guards in front of the tent circled to the back and sent that guard off on an errand. A moment later, the guard that had taken his place ran back to the front. Though he might only be gone for a moment, Beth had to take a chance to look inside the tent for Jonathan. Unless they had loaded him into one of the trucks, there was nowhere else he would be.

Hunkering low, she ran toward the tent, dropped to the ground and rolled up against the bottom edge. Once there, she hoped she could slide beneath the bottom edge. The gap wasn't wide enough for her to get her body beneath, but she could see inside.

A light shone down on a cot where a man lay, his trouser cut away from his leg.

Jonathan leaned over the cot, tending the man's wound.

Beth couldn't get to him, but at least she knew he was okay and where he was. She'd have to find a way to get him out of the tent and away from the terrorists. But first, she had to find a place to hide until she came up with a plan.

CHAPTER 12

THE TWO DELTA teams surrounded the compound tucked into the hills. By coming in over the top of a ridge, they were able to study the layout and locate the guards on the perimeter before moving in.

Bull, Lance and Blade took out the guards perched in the hills. Then the rest of the team moved in.

The compound was in a state of uproar as the terrorists hurried to break camp, load trucks and people to bug out. One tent remained standing in the middle of the camp. Everything else had been torn down and loaded.

"I'm going for the back of the tent," Dawg said.

"I've got your six," Rucker responded.

"We've got the guards on the front," Blade said into Dawg's headset.

"Charlie Team will work the rest. Go get the doc and nurse," Charlie team leader said.

As one, the teams moved in. With so much confusion, they were able to take out a number of the Boko Haram terrorists using knifes and stealth.

As Dawg and Rucker moved closer to the back of the big tent, a guard carrying an AK-47 left his position to go to the front where Blade, Bull and Lance were taking care of the guards there. Rucker went after the guy heading for the front while Dawg moved toward the back of the tent, hoping to find a doorway inside. Before he got there, a shadow moved from behind a barrel, and a figure stole up to the tent, dropped to the ground and looked beneath the edge.

His pulse picked up. The figure wasn't one of the Boko Haram, and it had a shape unlike any man in the compound. The most telling feature was the long hair hanging down from a ponytail.

Beth.

His first instinct was to rush forward, pull her into his arms and hold her tightly. But he couldn't risk exposing himself and her to the terrorists rushing around the compound. Instead, he eased up to where she lay on the ground, grabbed her from behind and clamped his hand over her mouth to keep her from crying out. She fought him, struggling to shake him off her back.

"Shh," he whispered. "It's me. Dawg."

Immediately, she stilled.

He removed his hand from her mouth, rolled off her and onto his feet. Still hunkered low, he pointed to the edge of the compound, indicating she should escape with him.

Beth shook her head and pointed to the tent. "Jonathan," she whispered so softly he barely heard what she said.

Shots were fired, and all hell broke loose.

"Got two of the guards," Rucker said. "Two ducked back into the tent. Sounds like Team Charlie has made contact."

"We have and could use some help."

Dawg pulled his knife from the scabbard on his hip. "Make some noise so I can get into this tent," he said into his mic.

He handed his nine millimeter pistol to Beth. "Can you?"

She nodded, flipped the safety off and held the gun in both hands.

A moment later, a loud explosion rocked the ground. At that moment, Dawg poked his knife through the canvas and ripped an opening large enough to allow him to enter. He dove inside and rolled to his feet. The guards that had entered the tent turned, weapons swinging toward him.

Dawg shot the first guy, took out the second

and was turning to look for more when another shot rang out. A guard standing on the other side of a cot in the middle of the room swayed and fell to the ground.

Dawg turned to find Beth beside him, his gun held tightly in her hands.

"Drop your weapons, or I shoot the doctor," a gravelly voice said from the cot.

The man lying there held a gun pointed at Colonel Parker's chest. His hand shook.

Colonel Parker swung his hand upward, knocking the gun from the wounded man's hand. It flew across the room and landed near Dawg's feet. "Count yourself lucky. I'd have let them shoot you, but I think you might provide valuable intel."

The sounds of gunfire continued, and truck engines revved as some of the terrorists made a run for it. Before long, the Deltas reported that they'd secured the site, and all the bad guys had been neutralized.

Black Hawk helicopters landed nearby. The wounded were loaded first, along with Colonel Parker, Beth and the Boko Haram leader, Kahbir.

Dawg didn't want to let Beth out of his sight, but he couldn't leave until all the Deltas could be transported out.

With their former base of operations nothing but ashes, they were flown to an airfield and out to Rota, Spain.

Dawg didn't see Beth again. The team was headed back to the States. He hoped he'd see her soon. Until then, he'd have to wonder if she'd still want to go out with him, or if she'd patched things up with her former fiancé.

EPILOGUE

BETH SCOURED THROUGH HER CLOSET, searching for something sexy, feminine and perfect for the night ahead.

"Girl, you have to wear something," Nora said. "Why not the red dress? It's as sexy as they come and makes a statement."

"What statement?"

"I want you to take this off me and make love to me all night long…?" Nora grinned. "That's what you want, right?"

"Yes. But shouldn't I be just a little more subtle?" She pulled the red dress out of the closet and stepped into it. The fabric slid up over hips, and she slipped her arms through the spaghetti straps. "I haven't seen him in two weeks. Do you think he will have changed his mind about me?"

"Not a chance. A woman who shoots first and

asks questions later is every man's wet dream." Nora hugged Beth. "I'm so glad you made it back home alive. I can't imagine the terror of being captured by the Boko Haram."

"I'm glad to be here, too." She hugged Nora back, and then spun away. "He'll be here any minute, and I'm not ready."

Nora dug in Beth's closet and came up with strappy silver stilettos. "Wear these. And turn around so I can zip you."

Beth turned, Nora zipped and the doorbell rang.

Her heart in her throat, Beth turned to Nora. "What do I do? What do I say?"

"Sweetie, you be yourself. That's what he loves about you." Nora nodded toward the door. "Go."

Beth drew in a shaky breath and walked to the door, threw it open and stood there in her bare feet and the sexy red dress.

On the other side, stood the man who'd been on her mind since she'd talked about dogs at the Salty Dog Saloon all those weeks ago. He wore a black suit with a red tie that matched her dress, and he was so handsome Beth wanted to cry.

"Hey," he said.

"Hey," she replied.

He reached out his hand. "You look like a million bucks."

She placed her hand in his. "You clean up pretty good yourself."

Dawg looked past her to Nora and nodded. "Thanks, Nora. I was hoping you'd get her into the red dress again."

Beth frowned. "You two making plans without me?"

Dawg shrugged. "I wanted our first real date to be perfect. I have reservations at the most expensive restaurant in town. But I'm giving you a choice. The restaurant or a grilled steak at my house."

She chewed on her bottom lip, her gaze sweeping over him from head to toe. "You look amazing. I hate that you went to all the trouble to take me to a fancy restaurant when I'd rather grill out at your place."

He grinned. "I thought you might say that. One of these days, I will get you to a real restaurant. But tonight, it's dinner at my place. And it's all arranged with fancy china, candles and music."

Nora squeezed past them. "I'll leave you two to it. Have fun."

Once Nora left, Dawg walked Beth back into her apartment, closed the door and pulled her into his arms.

Beth laughed and melted against him. "Are we starting with dessert?"

He nodded.

She didn't wait for him to initiate. Standing on her toes, she claimed his lips and opened to him, taking his tongue in a slow, sexy glide. "This is where I've wanted to be," she whispered against his lips.

"I've been counting the hours and minutes until I could see you again." He leaned his forehead against hers. "I think I'm in love."

"How can you know?"

He brushed a strand of her hair back from her cheek. "The thought of being without you breaks my heart."

"That's exactly how I feel. But is it too soon?"

"If it is, we'll give it more time. But I know in my soul you're the one for me," he said.

"And you're the one for me." She wrapped her arms around his neck and kissed him again.

This time when they came up for air, they laughed.

"Save some dessert for later," she said. "You owe me dinner."

"You've got it." He brushed a kiss across her lips. "And you've got me. Forever and always."

SEAL SALVATION

BROTHERHOOD PROTECTORS COLORADO
BOOK #1

New York Times & USA Today
Bestselling Author

ELLE JAMES

SEAL SALVATION

BROTHERHOOD PROTECTORS

Colorado

New York Times & USA Today Bestselling Author

ELLE JAMES

CHAPTER 1

JAKE COGBURN SAT in the tattered lounge chair he'd scavenged on the side of the street after moving into an empty apartment in Colorado Springs. He hadn't planned on living in an apartment, nor had he planned on sleeping on the only piece of furniture he could afford without digging into his savings. He'd put aside money to purchase a plot of land out in the middle of nowhere Colorado. On that land, he'd wanted to build a house.

All those plans had been blown away, along with the lower half of his left leg, when he'd stepped on an IED in Afghanistan. Yeah, he had the money in the bank, but what good did it do him? On one leg, what could he accomplish? Working a piece of land and building a house took all four limbs.

He poured another tumbler of whiskey and

tipped the contents up, letting the cool liquid burn a path down his throat. Soon, the numbing effect set in. Jake could almost forget the phantom pain in his missing leg, could almost forget he'd not only lost a leg, but had lost the only family he'd ever had.

As a Navy SEAL, his teammates had been his brothers. Every one of them would lay down his life for him, as he'd taken one for the team when his foot had landed on that IED.

Medically discharged, having gone through multiple surgeries and physical therapy, he'd been dumped out into a civilian world that had no use for a one-legged, former Navy SEAL.

What was he good for? His skillset included demolitions, tactical operations, highly effective weapons firing and hand-to-hand combat.

Where could he find that kind of work in a civilian occupation? And doing all that balanced on one leg?

Nope.

He was all washed up. His only hope was to sit on a corner with his hat held out, begging like a hundred other homeless veterans roaming the streets of Colorado Springs.

His free hand clenched into a fist. Jake had never begged for anything in his life. He'd fought for what he'd accomplished. From surviving the gangs on the streets of Denver, to forging his way through BUD/S training, he'd always counted on his mind and brute strength to get through any hardship.

But now…

Through the empty glass tumbler, he stared down at the stump below his left knee then slammed the glass against the wall. It hit hard and shattered into a million pieces that scattered across the floor.

A knock sounded on the door to his apartment.

"I didn't put a dent in the damned wall!" he yelled. "Leave me the fuck alone."

"Jake Cogburn?" An unfamiliar male voice called out from the other side of the faded wooden panel.

"Yeah," Jake muttered. "I'm not interested in buying anything."

"I'm not selling anything," the muffled voice sounded.

"Then get the fuck away from my door," Jake said and tipped the bottle of whiskey up, downing the last swallow. The bottle followed the glass, hitting the wall with a solid thump before it crashed to the wooden floor and bounced.

"Everything all right in there?" the man called out.

"Who the hell cares?" Jake muttered.

"I do."

Jake frowned. "I told you. I'm not buying anything."

"And I told you I'm not selling anything." A moment of silence followed. "Would you open the door for a brother?"

Anger surged through Jake. "I don't have a brother. I'm an only fuckin' child."

"Then how about a brother-in-arms? A fellow spec ops guy? A Delta Force man?"

Jake barked a single laugh. "Yeah. Yeah. Whatever. The SEALs don't operate out of Colorado. And as far as I know, there isn't a Delta Force unit near here."

"Not active Delta Force," the man fired back. "Look. A friend sent me to offer you a job."

"I don't have any friends," Jake said, then added muttering beneath his breath, "and I'm not fit for any jobs."

"You're fit for the job he's got in mind," the man said. "Look, Cog, the only easy day was yesterday. Are you a SEAL or not?"

Cog.

Only the men he'd fought with side by side had called him Cog.

A frown pulled his brow low as he leaned forward in his chair. "Anyone can look up the SEAL motto. How do I know you're the real deal?" Jake had to admit he was curious now.

"You have to trust me." The man chuckled. "It's not like us Deltas have tridents tattooed on our foreheads like you Navy SEALs. My honor was forged in battle, just like yours."

Despite himself, Jake's lips twitched. No, they didn't have tridents, the symbol of their trade, drawn in indelible ink on their foreheads. But it was etched into their hearts. The grueling training they'd survived had made them proud to wear the symbol of the Navy SEAL and even prouder to fight as a team alongside the Delta Force operatives.

"Who sent you?" Jake asked.

"Hank Patterson," the voice said and waited.

A flood of memories washed over Jake. Hank had been his mentor when he'd come on board, fresh from BUD/S training. He hadn't hazed him as the others on the team had. He'd taken Jake beneath his wing and taught him everything he knew that would help him in the many missions to come. Many of Hank's techniques had kept Jake alive on more than one occasion. He owed the man his life.

"Why didn't Hank come himself?" Jake asked.

"He and his wife have a new baby. You might not be aware that his wife is a famous actress. She's going on set in a few days, and Hank has diaper duty."

"Hank? Diaper duty?" Jake shook his head. The alcohol in his system made his vision blur. "Doesn't sound like Hank."

"Well, it is. Will you open the door so we can discuss his proposition?"

Jake glanced around the pathetic excuse of an apartment and shook his head. "No. But I'll come out in a minute. You can buy me a drink, and we can talk."

"Good," the man said. "Anything to get out of this hallway. Your neighbors are giving me threatening looks."

Jake reached for his prosthesis, pulled up his pantleg, donned the inner sleeve, slipped his stump into position and pulled the outer sleeve over his thigh. He slid his good foot into a shoe and pushed to a standing position, swaying slightly.

He smelled like dirty clothes and alcohol. But he'd be damned if he let Hank's emissary into the apartment to see how low Jake Cogburn had sunk.

Lifting his shirt up to his nose, he grimaced. Then he yanked it over his head, slung it across the room and reached into the duffel bag in the corner for another T-shirt.

The sniff test had him flinging that shirt across the room to land with the other in a heap on the floor. Two shirts later, he settled on a black Led Zeppelin T-shirt that had been a gift from one of his buddies on his last SEAL team. The man had been a fan of one of the biggest bands of the seventies, a time way before he'd been born.

Running a hand through his hair, he shoved his

socked-foot and his prosthetic foot into a pair of boots and finally opened the door.

The man on the other side leaned against the opposite wall in the hallway. He pushed away from the wall and held out his hand. "Jake Cogburn, I'm Joseph Kuntz. My friends call me Kujo."

Jake gave the man a narrow-eyed glare but took the hand. "What kind of job does Hank have in mind. Not that I'm interested." He shook the hand and let go quickly.

"He's started a business up in Montana and wants to open up a branch here in Colorado." Kujo ran his glance over Jake.

Jake's shoulders automatically squared. "And?"

"And he wants you to head it up."

Jake laughed out loud. "Hank wants this broken-down SEAL to head up an office?"

Kujo nodded. "He does."

"Why don't *you* do it?"

"I have a pregnant wife back in Montana. I only have a few weeks to help you lay the groundwork. Then I have to get back."

His head shaking back and forth, Jake stared at the man as if he'd lost his mind. "What the hell kind of business can a one-legged ex-SEAL manage? Does he even know me?"

"He said he mentored you as a newbie SEAL a long time back. He knows your service record and thinks you would make the perfect man to lead the new branch." Kujo crossed his arms over his chest. "He has confidence that you have the skills needed to do the job. And there's no such thing as an ex-SEAL. Once a SEAL, always a SEAL. "

Jake nodded. The man was right. "He knew me back then. But does he know me now?" Jake touched the thigh of his injured leg.

Kujo nodded. "He knows about your circumstances, and he's still certain you're the one to do the job."

Jake shook his head. "What exactly will this branch of his business sell?"

"We're a service organization. We provide security and unique skills to our clients to protect them and/or take care of situations law enforcement or the military might not be in a position to assist with."

"Vigilantes?" Kujo held up his hands. "No thanks."

"Not vigilantes," Kujo said. "More a security service for those in need of highly trained special ops folks who know how to handle a gun and run a tactical mission."

"Again," Jake said, "sounds like vigilantes. No thanks. Besides, I'm not fit to fight. The Navy told me so." He turned to go back into his apartment and find another whiskey glass.

Kujo stepped between him and the door. "Can you fire a weapon?"

Jake shrugged. "Sure. Nothing wrong with my hands and arms. But I can't run, jump and maneuver the way I used to before..." He tipped his chin toward his prosthesis.

"You still have a brain. You can compensate," Kujo raised his eyebrows. "Do you have a job?"

Jake's chest tightened. "No."

Kujo's chin lifted a fraction. "Then, what do you have to lose?" He stood with his shoulders back, his head held high—the way Jake used to stand.

What did he have to lose? He'd lost everything that had been important to him. He couldn't sink any lower. His brows furrowing, he stared into Kujo's open, friendly face and then shrugged. "I have nothing to lose."

Kujo nodded. "Trust me. I've been there. Hank Patterson brought me out of the hell I'd sunk into. Life has only gotten better since."

"Well, you have both legs," Jake pointed out.

"And you have your hands and mind, one perfectly good leg and a prosthetic device you can get around on just fine from what I can see." He frowned. "Are you going to stand around belly-aching or come with me and start a new job I think you'll love."

"I'm not bellyaching," Jake grumbled.

"But you're wasting daylight, and I have another place I need to be before dark." Kujo stood back. "What's it to be?"

For a tense moment, Jake stood fast. After weeks of wallowing in the hovel of an apartment, getting out seemed more difficult than staying with the familiar.

"Why did Hank choose me?" he asked.

"Based on your past performance as a Navy SEAL, Hank thought you were the right person for the task he had in mind. He trusts you, your work and your integrity. The job won't always be easy…" Kujo grinned. "But the only easy day…"

"Yeah, yeah…was yesterday." Jake impatiently waved Kujo ahead of him. "I'm coming. But don't take that as a yes. I have yet to decide whether I want to work for Hank."

Kujo cocked an eyebrow. "You have a better job offer?"

Jake wanted to tell the man that he did, but he couldn't. "No."

"Fine. Come with me. We have another stop to make before we seal this deal and kick off this project." Kujo nodded toward the interior of the apartment. "Got a go bag?"

Jake glanced back. "Not since I left the service. Why?"

"We'll most likely stay the night where we're going. Maybe longer. Grab what you need for a couple of days."

Jake returned to his apartment, grabbed the duffel bag out of the bottom of the closet and stuffed a pair of jeans, socks, underwear, some T-shirts, a jacket and his shaving kit into it. He returned to his apartment entrance where Kujo waited.

The other man stepped outside and waited for Jake to follow.

Jake carried his bag through the door and pulled it closed behind him. "Where are we going?"

"To a ranch."

His feet coming to an immediate halt, Jake shook his head. "Why are we going to a ranch? You didn't say anything about a ranch."

Kujo drew in a deep breath and let it go slowly, as if he was holding back his own impatience. "Bear with me. I'll fill you in when we get there. Just suffice it to say, your job will be important to someone."

"Who?"

Kujo grinned. "Whoever needs you most."

"That's kind of vague, if you ask me."

"It's the nature of the work," Kujo said.

"Just what exactly does this job entail?" Jake asked.

"Don't worry." Kujo led the way down the stairs of the apartment complex and out to a shiny, black SUV. "I fully intend to brief you on your position and the nature of Hank's organization. But first, I'd like to get out of here and up into the mountains."

Jake climbed into the SUV, silently cursing his

prosthetic when it banged against the door. Once in his seat, he buckled his seatbelt, wondering what the hell he was doing and when the hell he'd get that drink Kujo promised. Thankfully, he hadn't committed to anything, which was his only saving grace. What kind of job could Hank have in mind for a one-legged, former Navy SEAL?

SEAL Salvation

ABOUT THE AUTHOR

ELLE JAMES also writing as MYLA JACKSON is a *New York Times* and *USA Today* Bestselling author of books including cowboys, intrigues and paranormal adventures that keep her readers on the edges of their seats. When she's not at her computer, she's traveling, snow skiing, boating, or riding her ATV, dreaming up new stories. Learn more about Elle James at www.ellejames.com

Website | Facebook | Twitter | GoodReads | Newsletter | BookBub | Amazon

Or visit her alter ego Myla Jackson at mylajackson.com
Website | Facebook | Twitter | Newsletter

Follow Me!
www.ellejames.com
ellejames@ellejames.com

Marine's Promise (#3)

SEAL's Vow (#4)

Warrior's Resolve (#5)

Brotherhood Protectors Series

Montana SEAL (#1)

Bride Protector SEAL (#2)

Montana D-Force (#3)

Cowboy D-Force (#4)

Montana Ranger (#5)

Montana Dog Soldier (#6)

Montana SEAL Daddy (#7)

Montana Ranger's Wedding Vow (#8)

Montana SEAL Undercover Daddy (#9)

Cape Cod SEAL Rescue (#10)

Montana SEAL Friendly Fire (#11)

Montana SEAL's Mail-Order Bride (#12)

SEAL Justice (#13)

Ranger Creed (#14)

Delta Force Rescue (#15)

Dog Days of Christmas (#16)

Montana Rescue (Sleeper SEAL)

Hot SEAL Salty Dog (SEALs in Paradise)

Hot SEAL,Hawaiian Nights (SEALs in Paradise)

Hot SEAL Bachelor Party (SEALs in Paradise)

Hot SEAL, Independence Day (SEALs in Paradise)

Brotherhood Protectors Vol 1

The Outrider Series

Homicide at Whiskey Gulch (#1)

Hideout at Whiskey Gulch (#2)

Hellfire Series

Hellfire, Texas (#1)

Justice Burning (#2)

Smoldering Desire (#3)

Hellfire in High Heels (#4)

Playing With Fire (#5)

Up in Flames (#6)

Total Meltdown (#7)

Declan's Defenders

Marine Force Recon (#1)

Show of Force (#2)

Full Force (#3)

Driving Force (#4)

Tactical Force (#5)

Disruptive Force (#6)

Mission: Six

One Intrepid SEAL

Two Dauntless Hearts

Three Courageous Words

Four Relentless Days

Five Ways to Surrender

Six Minutes to Midnight

Hearts & Heroes Series

Wyatt's War (#1)

Mack's Witness (#2)

Ronin's Return (#3)

Sam's Surrender (#4)

Take No Prisoners Series

SEAL's Honor (#1)

SEAL'S Desire (#2)

SEAL's Embrace (#3)

SEAL's Obsession (#4)

SEAL's Proposal (#5)

SEAL's Seduction (#6)

SEAL'S Defiance (#7)

SEAL's Deception (#8)

SEAL's Deliverance (#9)

SEAL's Ultimate Challenge (#10)

Texas Billionaire Club

Tarzan & Janine (#1)

Something To Talk About (#2)

Who's Your Daddy (#3)

Love & War (#4)

Billionaire Online Dating Service

The Billionaire Husband Test (#1)

The Billionaire Cinderella Test (#2)

The Billionaire Bride Test (#3)

The Billionaire Daddy Test (#4)

The Billionaire Matchmaker Test (#5)

The Billionaire Glitch Date (#6)

The Billionaire Perfect Date (#7) coming soon

The Billionaire Replacement Date (#8) coming soon

The Billionaire Wedding Date (#9) coming soon

Ballistic Cowboy

Hot Combat (#1)

Hot Target (#2)

Hot Zone (#3)

Hot Velocity (#4)

Cajun Magic Mystery Series

Voodoo on the Bayou (#1)

Voodoo for Two (#2)

Deja Voodoo (#3)

Cajun Magic Mysteries Books 1-3

SEAL Of My Own

Navy SEAL Survival

Navy SEAL Captive

Navy SEAL To Die For

Navy SEAL Six Pack

Devil's Shroud Series

Deadly Reckoning (#1)

Deadly Engagement (#2)

Deadly Liaisons (#3)

Deadly Allure (#4)

Deadly Obsession (#5)

Deadly Fall (#6)

Covert Cowboys Inc Series

Triggered (#1)

Taking Aim (#2)

Bodyguard Under Fire (#3)

Cowboy Resurrected (#4)

Navy SEAL Justice (#5)

Navy SEAL Newlywed (#6)

High Country Hideout (#7)

Clandestine Christmas (#8)

Thunder Horse Series

Hostage to Thunder Horse (#1)

Thunder Horse Heritage (#2)

Thunder Horse Redemption (#3)

Christmas at Thunder Horse Ranch (#4)

Demon Series

Hot Demon Nights (#1)

Demon's Embrace (#2)

Tempting the Demon (#3)

Lords of the Underworld

Witch's Initiation (#1)

Witch's Seduction (#2)

The Witch's Desire (#3)

Possessing the Witch (#4)

Stealth Operations Specialists (SOS)

Nick of Time

Alaskan Fantasy

Boys Behaving Badly Anthology

Rogues (#1)

Blue Collar (#2)